"Why Have You Held Out Against Me for So Long, Angela?"

Paul murmured, his lips warm against her cheek.

She swallowed. "Because—I—I must—"

"Must is a word I'd take out of your vocabulary," Paul said softly. "Unless it's to say that you must listen to your heart."

"Is that what you're doing?" Angela said unsteadily.

"Of course. From the first moment I saw you no one else existed for me, my darling."

The blood flowed more quickly to her veins as he called her his darling. It was what she wanted . . . to be his, now and for always. . . .

JEAN SAUNDERS

describes herself as a compulsive writer and has written 23 novels and over 600 short stories. A participating member of several British writers' organizations including the Romantic Novelists Association, Jean enjoys anything to do with writing and writers.

Dear Reader:

Silhouette has always tried to give you exactly what you want. When you asked for increased realism, deeper characterization and greater length, we brought you Silhouette Special Editions. When you asked for increased sensuality, we brought you Silhouette Desire. Now you ask for books with the length and depth of Special Editions, the sensuality of Desire, but with something else besides, something that no one else offers. Now we bring you SILHOUETTE INTIMATE MOMENTS, true romance novels, longer than the usual, with all the depth that length requires. More sensuous than the usual, with characters whose maturity matches that sensuality. Books with the ingredient no one else has tapped: excitement.

There is an electricity between two people in love that makes everything they do magic, larger than life—and this is what we bring you in SILHOUETTE INTIMATE MOMENTS. Look for them this May, wherever you buy books.

These books are for the woman who wants more than she has ever had before. These books are for you. As always, we look forward to your comments and suggestions. You can write to me at the address below:

Karen Solem
Editor-in-Chief
Silhouette Books
P.O. Box 769
New York, N.Y. 10019

JEAN SAUNDERS
Love's Sweet Music

Silhouette *Romance*
Published by Silhouette Books New York
America's Publisher of Contemporary Romance

Other Silhouette Books by Jean Saunders

The Kissing Time

SILHOUETTE BOOKS, a Simon & Schuster Division of
GULF & WESTERN CORPORATION
1230 Avenue of the Americas, New York, N.Y. 10020

Distributed by Pocket Books

ISBN: 0-671-57216-4

First Silhouette Books printing April, 1983

10 9 8 7 6 5 4 3 2 1

Map by Ray Lundgren

America's Publisher of Contemporary Romance

Printed in the U.S.A.

Love's Sweet Music

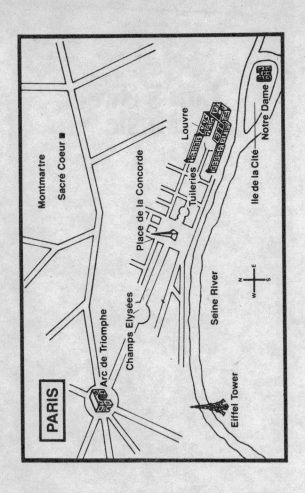

Chapter One

The memory of the interview with Charlie Cass of the Cass Music Agency kept recurring as Angela methodically emptied the chest of drawers in her half of the bedroom she shared with Lorna.

Not that it had been a very long interview. Once Charlie Cass knew that she'd had experience in public relations with a minor politician and was prepared to travel as soon as Paul Blake's concert tour got underway, she was hired.

Angela's heart still skipped a beat every time she realized she was actually going to be traveling through France as Paul Blake's personal assistant. She was quite a fan of his, and he was the one thing that she and Lorna totally disagreed upon. Angela was a devotee of classical music, while Lorna preferred jazz and country.

Angela leaned back on her heels and paused in the sorting of clothes and hoarded knickknacks. Her eyes grew dreamy, despite the fact that the first meeting with Paul Blake had been slightly traumatic. He still had a charisma about him that was undeniable. . . .

She'd been aware of his music long before she was aware of the man, of course. His particular piano-playing style was almost sensual. Listening to him play, it sounded as if he caressed the keys lovingly, the way a man might caress a woman. . . .

Angela shivered. To someone of her sensitivity, his

style told a lot about the man. Through his music, she had always felt she knew him already. He was a man of changing moods, as was anyone with a strongly artistic temperament, with the flair to interpret every piece as the composer intended, and yet still manage to give it something of himself.

Her thoughts returned to the interview. Charlie Cass explained the duties of personal assistant to Paul Blake succinctly; she would organize the press interviews and the TV boys; arrange hotel bookings and plane tickets; hire cars when necessary; keep unwanted admirers and autograph hunters away from Paul's dressing room, and generally be at the Great One's beck and call. In other words, she thought dryly, paid slavery—but, she had to admit, very well paid. She was unable to resist a touch of sarcasm when the agent finally finished speaking.

"I don't suppose he'll want me to wipe his nose as well?"

She sensed the click of the door closing behind her almost before she heard it.

"I don't think that will be necessary. I came out of kindergarten some time ago, Miss Raines."

At the sound of the new voice, Angela's head jerked around. She'd have known it was Paul Blake even if she hadn't recognized him from the record sleeves. She felt her face flood with color, and was furious with herself because of it. For a few seconds she couldn't think of a single thing to say as his gaze held hers, and the vivid instant impression of his forceful personality had stayed with her long after she left the poky little office.

She had seen photographs of Paul Blake. His face had smiled at her from posters and record sleeves. She even had a couple of his LPs; but on the covers there had usually been a head-and-shoulders portrait of a dark-haired man in evening dress, always with a crisp white bow tie at his neck, and a red rose in his buttonhole.

The inanimate pictures had never captured the deep, velvet brown of his eyes or the little laughter lines at their corners. Angela felt the pulse beating in her throat as she registered the difference between the publicity photos and the real man.

The photos had flattened his nose, which was long enough to make him stern if it hadn't been for the smiling mouth below. She'd studied his picture quite often, so she should have been prepared for that very sensual mouth. But no picture could have done justice to the richly tanned skin, on which there was the faintest hint of dark shadow that afternoon of the interview—a shadow that only added to Paul Blake's sensuality.

No man had any right to be that dishy and have talent too, Lorna had drooled the first time she'd seen his picture, even if it wasn't the kind of talent in which she was interested.

Angela ran her tongue over her dry lips on the day she came face to face with him in Charlie Cass's office. He appeared unexpectedly, and the smiling facade he usually put on for the public was nowhere to be seen. Instead, Paul stared at her coolly, his eyes moving almost languorously over her shape. She was wearing an apricot colored linen suit for the interview, and Paul Blake's gaze paused at all the interesting places for a fraction too long, so that she felt like a specimen under the microscope of his scrutiny. His glance lingered on her slim legs and the shiny bronze high-heeled shoes that gave her added height. *It was a look that stripped her naked*, she thought angrily, and knew it was designed to unnerve her.

Paul Blake was very different in the flesh from his cardboard charm, she realized at once. Recognizable, but different. For one thing, the record-sleeve pictures had given no clue as to his height. He was taller than she'd imagined, slim-hipped in sand-colored corduroy slacks, his shoulders broad inside his cream rollneck sweater. Altogether, he was an athletic-looking man, without the slight stoop of the shoulders some older professional pianists acquired.

He was also younger than Angela had expected. She'd always guessed that the record companies had touched up the photographs for his public image. She had been in the public relations game too long not to know how much of that sort of thing went on. But in Paul Blake's case, he'd been portrayed pretty accurately. *How old then,* she wondered? Early thirties, maybe a little more. The kind of man many women would fall for at once. And the way he was staring at her in Charlie Cass's office, with that brooding aggressive look in his eyes, only added to his masculinity.

She kicked herself for her unthinking comment, still trying to think of a suitable reply to his retort. She could hardly have gotten off to a worse start with a prospective employer. And then he spoke again, his rich voice clearly under tight control.

"And what makes Miss Angela Raines think a spell of work in a politician's employ makes her the ideal personal assistant for me?"

Angela caught the little movement as the agent flicked a button on a small plastic machine just visible in the open drawer of his desk. She hadn't noticed it until now.

"You were listening in!" She accused Paul Blake now, too outraged at the realization to bother about being polite. She was quickly abandoning the idea of working for him anyway. It had seemed a marvelous chance until a few moments ago, when some sixth sense told her it was going to be very wearing on the nerves, emotionally as well as physically.

He might as well know right away that she didn't approve of such underhanded methods. She hated still more the fact that he'd overheard everything she'd said in the past fifteen minutes while he hid away in some

10

little cubbyhole to listen. Including her unguarded admission that she adored his music. She glared at him, and to her surprise he began to laugh.

Angela felt her cheeks burn, even though he wasn't laughing at her. It was a rich warm companionable laugh that seemed to come from deep inside him. It changed his face and his entire personality, and seemed to establish a sudden intimacy between them, as if they shared a secret. Her mouth was still dry as the first faint shock waves of attraction touched her, despite herself.

She realized that Paul's whole face came alive when he laughed. The little lines at the sides of his brown eyes deepened, and dancing lights heightened the velvet softness of them. His jawline, too, was gentler as the wide mouth curved upward, shortening his long face. He was ruggedly handsome when he smiled, the coldness gone, the warmth reaching out to her almost tangibly. He crossed the room to her in two easy strides, his hand stretched out to grasp hers.

As she expected, they were beautiful hands. Pianist's hands, with long tapering fingers, slim and well manicured, but in no way effeminate. That was one word which would never be applied to Paul Blake. She realized that her heart was thudding erratically, and she tried to remain cool and distant as he apologized. She couldn't be sure whether he was being too effusive or not.

"It's a terrible habit I have," he informed her. "Charlie says I'm going to hear something really bad about myself one of these days, but I can't resist trying to picture the person speaking, and matching him or her to the voice."

Angela rose to the bait.

"And do I match the voice?"

The hand that still held hers tightened imperceptibly; his fingers moving so slightly against her own that she might almost have imagined it.

11

"Oh, I'd say you complemented it perfectly, Miss Raines. I imagined a young lady of considerable charm to go with that gentle voice."

Oh, was he ever smooth when he wanted to be, Angela thought. He was too used to paying compliments to be entirely trusted. He was a ladies' man, and she mistrusted him instinctively, particularly when she saw the small knowing smile on Charlie Cass's plump face as he tilted back his swivel chair. He had a look that said all the ladies fell under Paul Blake's spell sooner or later, and he didn't expect the new p.a. to be any different. Angela removed her hand with a deft movement.

"This gentle voice can carry a sting when it needs to," she said coolly, and the laugh changed to a mock grimace.

"Don't I know it," Paul commented. "I decided to make my presence known as soon as I heard the little bit of sarcasm creeping in, before you had a chance to talk yourself out of the job."

Her ruffled feelings relaxed a little. "You still want me then, in spite of that?" she asked lightly.

"I still want you." He wasn't laughing any more, though there was the hint of a smile on his lips, and Angela felt uneasily that he wasn't just referring to the job.

It was Paul who took over the interview from then on, as if Charlie Cass wasn't there. He spoke on a more personal level, discussing details of the forthcoming tour and the planned itinerary. Angela knew without doubt that it was going to be the most interesting job she'd ever undertaken.

Finally, Paul told her he'd leave Charlie Cass to sort out the financial details and he'd see her at Heathrow Airport on the fourth of August. Charlie would inform her of the time of departure in a few days' time. He held out his hand to her again; and as she clasped it, feeling the tingling where his fingers squeezed hers,

Angela accepted the inescapable fact that there was a magnetism about him. The office seemed oddly empty after he had left it; the sound of his voice still lingered in her head; and the almost desperate certainty in her mind, that the attraction between them was instant and mutual, made her doubt the wisdom of becoming part of his entourage after all.

Charlie Cass cleared his throat and looked at her, an ugly flush rising up his neck. If Angie had had any nervousness at this interview, it had been dispelled completely by the fact that this weaselly little man had been transmitting the discussion to Paul Blake's waiting ears. She glared at him angrily, her hazel eyes flashing.

"That was a dirty trick to play! Do you leave the intercom switched on with all your clients?"

"No," he admitted. "But Paul's special. Anyway, I was sure you were the right one for him, Angela. You don't mind if I call you Angela, do you? I knew as soon as he saw you there wouldn't be any problems."

She looked at him warily. "I'd like to know exactly what you mean by that," she said at last.

Charlie Cass shrugged. "Paul's got quite a way with the ladies, as you may have noticed. They usually fall in love with him sooner or later. It goes with the job. It's not the screaming adoration the pop stars get, but he has his stage-door followers, and you'll be expected to deal with them."

His oily gaze followed the same trail as Mr. Blake's, only this time it made her want to squirm.

"It helps to have a pretty young personal assistant," he said smoothly. "They'll assume you're Paul's girl-friend as well as his p.a., and if we're lucky they'll soon get fed up with pestering him when they see you around. In fact, if you want to warn them off with a hint to that effect, it's up to you; but you'd better be careful not to let the press get wind of it, or it's likely to be in all the gossip columns before you can say Rimski-Korsakov. I seem to recall your saying you had no attachments, which is just as well—though it surprises me with your looks, Angela."

His leering smile was probably supposed to be complimentary, but Angie was too infuriated to take any notice of it. Of all the nerve! It sounded as if she'd been hired mainly because of her appearance, to help ward off the attentions of overly amorous females out for a glimpse of their idol! It didn't do her ego one bit of good.

She was contemptuous of Paul Blake's assumption of his attraction to women, dismissing from her mind the fact that she was probably every bit as susceptible as the next one. As Lorna said—all that and talent too. For a second she was tempted to tell Charlie Cass what he could do with the job, but she knew she'd be a fool to turn down the chance to travel all over France, just because of the agent's smarmy words. They might not even be completely true; and besides, this tour might lead to others. Why should she assume Paul Blake would even make a play for her, anyway?

She gave a small shiver. At any rate, she was now forewarned. She'd make darned sure she wasn't added to the list of females who fell for Paul Blake's brand of charm. Her feet were staying firmly on the ground as far as he was concerned.

"Who else will be traveling with us?" she ignored everything else the agent had said, and spoke in a businesslike voice.

"No one," he said, to her dismay. "Paul loathes the idea of a gang of hangers-on trailing around with him, which is why it's so important to find the right person to be his p.a., and why he's prepared to pay such a high salary. If his last one hadn't decided to marry a Texas oilman at a minute's notice, we wouldn't be in such a flap now. But you've come to the rescue like an angel of mercy——"

Before he could make some facile comment about

her name, she cut him short and rose to leave, saying she'd look forward to hearing from him about the departure time on the fourth of August. She went down the narrow staircase to the warmth of the summer afternoon, feeling a little as if she'd emerged unscathed from an earthquake. *But for how long?* she wondered.

In the distance, a church clock struck, and Angela roused herself. It didn't change anything, no matter how often she went over the interview and her first meeting with Paul Blake. And now that it was all settled, there was too much to do in the flat to waste time daydreaming. She rummaged in the chest of drawers with a feeling of disbelief; she hadn't realized just how much of a hoarder she'd become. She pressed her cheek against the cool sheen of an evening top that had seen better days, remembering that the last time she'd worn it Tim had asked her to marry him yet again. She tossed the silvery top resolutely into the throwaway box. What use was a silver evening top with picks in it, anyway?

Lorna found her still browsing through the contents of the bureau, taking far longer than she should because she really hated to throw anything away—things or people. Lorna's eyes took in the jumble of clothes and boxes, and the little mementos that were Angie's stock-in-trade, and she felt a stab of regret. They'd had two happy years at the Kensington flat, and though it wouldn't be difficult to find another flatmate, there'd never be another one quite like Angie.

Warm, impulsive, lovely . . . Angela's name suited her looks, Lorna reflected. The face of an angel, with gold-brown hair that had the texture of warm silk, framing an oval face with a smooth, creamy complexion that Lorna envied. And those clear, hazel-colored eyes could look at you with disarming candor, yet smolder and darken with passion and anger. A soft, mobile mouth that was generously wide, and the appearance of too much perfection was relieved by the pert little nose that was just a little too retroussé.

"Do you think you'll know me again?" Angela's voice came from the depths of the throw-away box as she decided that the blue cashmere sweater was just too good to be discarded after all.

She couldn't take everything with her, though. Half of this stuff was going to have to stay in storage until she knew whether the job was going to be permanent—or if she'd have to take up Lorna's suggestion that the new flatmate must come on a temporary basis in case it all fell through.

"You really are going then," Lorna said unnecessarily.

Angela gave a low groan. "No! I'm just doing all this for the fun of it! Are you crazy? I didn't go through the interview with Paul's agent and then the drama of meeting the Great One himself just to say, no thanks, I don't want the job!"

"All right, I'm convinced. Anyway, I'm green with envy."

Angela's laugh caught in her throat. She was going to miss the easy relationship she and Lorna had shared, but the restlessness had been bothering her for months now. That, coupled with Tim's persistent proposals, had resolved her to take this step. Even if it did feel a little like a step into the unknown, she'd always wanted to travel, and this was the ideal opportunity. She'd be a fool to miss it.

"You wouldn't last a week and you know it," she told Lorna now. "You hate classical music for a start, so a fat lot of good you'd be to a concert pianist. I'll be expected to attend every concert, you know, and probably rehearsals too. Being a personal assistant doesn't mean sitting at a desk all day long. You couldn't fake an interest and get away with it for long."

"For the chance of a foreign tour with Paul Blake, I'd

16

fake anything." She grinned. "Especially if he's as dishy as you say. Have you told Tim the news yet, or is it going to be a big surprise when he gets back from his sales conference?"

Angela felt her heart give a small leap. She'd told Tim repeatedly that she couldn't marry him, knowing she just didn't love him the way a woman should love her husband. She certainly felt a great fondness for him, but her pulse didn't race every time she heard his voice, and the emotions he stirred in her were more what she'd feel toward an elder brother. As yet she was untouched by the deep love which she knew instinctively she was capable of giving, though Tim Harper hadn't been the one to unleash it.

He'd been part of her life for a long time, and she knew she was in for a sticky scene with him when she told him of her plans to leave England. Although it was only for two months to begin with, if she was a success on this tour, she would become the permanent personal assistant to Paul Blake. The French tour was to be a trial period on both sides. It had been providential that the job had come up while Tim was away, that applicants had to be prepared to leave almost at once, and that the interview had gone smoothly, so that she had been offered and had accepted the job before she really had time to consider Tim's reaction. And before he had the chance to try to sway her.

"I'm not married to Tim," she said shortly to Lorna. But despite her words she was ridiculously consumed with guilt because she was going to hurt his feelings, and angry with herself for feeling that way.

"In other words, you haven't told him yet," Lorna stated.

"What chance have I had——"

"He's phoned you every night. If you'd wanted him to know you had every opportunity to tell him on the phone instead of having to say it face to face, if it's bothering you that much."

Oh, she'd considered it. That would have been the easy way, but Angela knew she owed him more than that. He'd spent more than a year loving her, believing that one of these days she was going to give in and marry him. And he was too nice a person to run out on, though she told herself that was ridiculous too. She wasn't running out on Tim, and she wasn't taking this p.a. job as an escape.

"I'll see him tonight," she told Lorna matter-of-factly. "He gets back from Scarborough this afternoon, and I'll tell him then. Do you want this blue sweater? It's either you or Oxfam," she added, switching the conversation neatly.

Lorna said she'd take the sweater to remember her by, because as soon as Angela was in her glamorous new job, she'd forget all about her old friend.

"Don't be an idiot. I'll write and tell you everything," Angela promised. "Anyway, Paul Blake may look dishy on his record sleeves, but our short acquaintance wasn't exactly scintillating, remember? We almost took an instant dislike to each other."

"Oh, yes? Why did he hire you, then? And why did you accept?" Lorna retorted disbelievingly. Anyway, the man must have been wearing blinkers to take a dislike to Angie. She was every man's idea of the cuddly cutie.

"Because no one else answered the ad, and he needed someone urgently, that's why. The agent decided I was suitable—though if I'd had two heads I'd have been suitable, judging by the desperation on his face—so that was that."

"You still haven't said why you didn't tell him to get lost if you disliked him so much," Lorna persisted.

Angie glared at her. "Why don't you be a sweetie and make us some coffee instead of giving me the third degree? You won't have the chance to do it much longer, and I'm going to have to finish this tomorrow. I haven't got time to do it now with you nattering away."

Lorna took the hint, though Angela knew she would have had plenty of time if she hadn't sat there dreaming about Paul Blake half the afternoon, alternately thrilling to the idea of traveling and working with him, and remembering with fury the way he'd eavesdropped on her interview with Charlie Cass. She shrugged. She was probably making a fuss about nothing. When Lorna brought the two mugs of coffee back to the bedroom, she handed over a skirt Lorna had been eyeing for ages, and the slightly ruffled atmosphere between them disappeared.

She glanced at her watch. Tim would be arriving in less than an hour, and she needed to rehearse what she was going to say to him. Thank goodness Lorna was going out, because she suddenly felt nervous—a feeling she'd never known when Tim was around before.

As soon as he arrived he caught her up in his arms and kissed her. And as usual, it was like being kissed by someone very dear and familiar . . . like a big brother. The thought embarrassed her, when she knew perfectly well that Tim had very different ideas about her. He'd brought her a wall poster that said "Love Is . . . Being with You," which embarrassed her even more because of what she had to tell him. And as she expected, he took it badly.

While she delivered her news, she watched the smile fade from his good-looking face, and a look of incredulity replace it. His blue eyes darkened as he held her shoulders tightly.

"You're not serious, Angie?"

Suddenly he irritated her. Neither Tim nor Lorna, nor anyone else she'd spoken to about the new job, had taken her seriously right away. She spoke more sharply than she intended.

"Of course I'm serious. I've been for the interview, and I leave for Paris on the fourth of August. I don't know how I can make it any plainer, Tim!"

His round face went a dull red color.

"With Paul Blake," he said. "I hope it's not going to be just the two of you." There was a sudden look of suspicion in his eyes.

Angela wished she could say it wasn't just the two of them, that Charlie Cass and a whole coachload of hangers-on would be accompanying them. It sounded too cozy to admit to Tim how it really was.

"Well, I can't say I like the sound of this at all!"

Angela had never realized before just how pompous he could be when he set his mind to it. She reminded herself that he was naturally hurt at the thought of her going away, and counted to ten before she answered.

"Don't try to make it sound as if I'm going into white slavery, Tim," she said shortly. "Paul Blake will be my boss, remember, and from the sound of things I'm going to be kept very busy. He probably won't see me as a person at all, just as his employee."

"Nobody could help seeing you for what you are," Tim said abruptly, "and that's a very beautiful and desirable girl. Men of his sort are just the type to take advantage of someone as vulnerable as you——"

"Oh, Tim, honestly!" Angie began to laugh helplessly, because he was acting more like the outraged brother now than the ardent lover he'd prefer to be. "I'm not a complete idiot, you know. I'm quite capable of taking care of myself. Don't you think I am?"

For a few seconds he didn't answer, and then he pulled her roughly into his arms and smothered her face with kisses. She felt suddenly claustrophobic in his embrace.

"How many times do I have to tell you I want to take care of you, Angie?" Tim begged her. "Darling, don't go on this foolhardy job. Stay here and marry me. You can ring up this Blake guy and tell him you've changed your mind——"

"I can't, Tim——"

"You belong here!" He went on relentlessly. "This is

your home. Why do you want to go traipsing all over France at somebody's beck and call? Marry me, Angie. We'll have a houseful of babies if you like, then you won't have time to feel bored!"

Angela listened to him, knowing that he was pushing the possibility of marrying him further away with every word he spoke. Yes, she wanted to marry and have children—but there was more to it than that, and she was seeing it so clearly now. She needed to marry the right man, the one who could send her senses reeling with his touch, her heart leaping at the sound of his voice. .... The father of her unborn children had to be a very special man, not one who saw her as some kind of earth mother just waiting to be surrounded by fat contented babies to keep her at home. She pushed Tim gently away from her.

"I can't marry you, Tim," she told him clearly. "I don't know how else to say it. I love you—but not enough to marry you, and you have to accept it. Please don't let us part on bad terms after all this time."

"How else can we part?" he said sulkily. "All this time, as you put it, I suppose I've just been wasting my life, waiting for you to make up your mind; and now you throw it all back in my face."

"That's not fair," Angela said tightly. "I've always been honest with you. If you just didn't listen, then you have only yourself to blame."

It was true, but it was a painful scene all the same. Angela was glad when he said he wouldn't stay for the evening after all, and he was sure she had plenty of things to do to prepare for her new life. She tried not to feel bitter after he'd gone, but maybe it was better for him to be angry than to suffer the pangs of a broken heart. Somehow Angie thought he'd survive. She made herself a mug of coffee once she was alone, and switched on the television to stop herself from thinking about Tim too much.

It was some inane comedy program, and she

switched to another channel. She didn't feel like being "entertained" by banal jokes tonight. She'd checked the lineup of the evening's programs, and saw at once an item merely labeled "Concert."

She remembered Charlie Cass's parting remark after the interview in his office. "If you've never seen Paul perform, there'll be a repeat performance of one of his concerts at the Albert Hall on television Friday evening. I'm sure you'd enjoy it."

She'd half intended to watch it and then forgot all about it until now. She *should* watch it, of course. If she was going to work for the man, she should be familiar with the way he performed and the kind of music he played. She only knew that he didn't play just the really heavy stuff, but preferred the popular classics, and she'd read somewhere that he was adept at giving a popular song the classic treatment. Yes, of course she should tune in to the program.

She was talking herself into it as if some hidden force was pushing her on, Angela thought irritably. But at ten o'clock she sat expectantly in front of the television screen, feeling her interest quicken as Paul Blake's name came up in a scrawled signature she assumed to be his—a carelessly scrawled name, in the way of people who didn't need to take too much trouble, because they'd be instantly recognized anyway. Angela's lips pursed together slightly. It was what she would have expected, having met him.

The orchestra was already in position, and Angela felt the excitement of the audience transmitted to her. There was a brief lull, and then a storm of applause as a tall figure in evening dress walked out to the platform, a red rose in his buttonhole, his face smiling and alight with pleasure at the response to his appearance. *No wonder they adore him,* Angela thought. He showed none of the egotism she'd encountered in the agent's office. He was in his own environment, ready and eager to give the audience what they had come for, and in the next hour Angela sat enthralled as she watched Paul perform.

It wasn't so much a concert as an experience. He lived every nuance of the music in his chosen pieces, his face reflecting the concentration needed for the mind-bending dexterity of the "Flight of the Bumblebee" to the gentleness and delicacy of Mendelssohn's "On Wings of Song."

Poignant melody filled the vast hall, and the camera closed in to give a close-up of the pianist's face. Angela thought she would probably never have a better chance to study it. In profile, he was like a Greek god, with a long straight nose and dark hair curling just above the whiteness of his shirt collar. He had a strong profile, the chin firm and taut, but when the camera angle moved slowly round to show him full-face, Angela could see the dreaminess in his eyes as his fingers played expertly over the keys.

Those eyes, which had been so cold and condemning when he'd thought she was sneering at him in the agent's office, were softer now. Soft as the brown velvet she'd likened them to, and the corners of his mouth were uptilted. The camera followed his sensitive fingers caressing the keys. Long and mobile, they soothed the keys the way a man seduced a woman, subtly and tenderly. Angie realized she was breathing more quickly, wondering for a moment just how it would feel to have those hands holding her. . . .

The concert was coming to an end. Paul looked right into the camera. It seemed as if he looked directly into her eyes as he said that he was going to finish the concert with a classical version of "Autumn Leaves." Though not a classical piece in the grand style of Mozart or Mendelssohn, the piece had produced such acclaim over the years since its introduction to the music world that it was frequently used in concert repertoires. It lent itself perfectly to a light, romantic version in which the lyrics were poignant and sad; or to a thrilling classical interpretation, which Paul Blake was now playing.

Angela felt her eyes blur a little as he gave it the concert pianist treatment. For a moment she had the craziest feeling that he must have known it was one of her favorite tunes, and that he'd done this deliberately —but of course he hadn't. The concert had been recorded several months ago, and this was a repeat broadcast. This performance had been filmed long before he met her, so it was nothing more than a coincidence.

She watched as the cameramen did a bit of TV trickery, rotating around the platform and putting several images of Paul's straight back on the screen as his fingers rippled over the keys in the special arrangement of "Autumn Leaves." The original French version was by Joseph Kosma, but the English lyrics that had turned it into a more familiar piece were running through her head, despite the crashing chords and minor-key embellishments beloved of classical compositions.

The words of the song spoke of summer kisses and nights that were long and cold. . . . Angie suddenly shivered. Paul's face was in focus on the screen now, so close that she felt she could reach out and touch it. His smile for the camera was warm and intimate, as if he sang the words inside himself too. Maybe he did. Maybe there was someone special in his life for whom the words had a personal meaning. It didn't matter to her. It wasn't going to matter to her.

But long after the concert was finished and she had turned off the TV, it was that particular piece of music that still lived inside her head. She couldn't rid herself of its haunting.

In bed, she pretended to be asleep when Lorna came home, because she didn't want to break the spell of the evening by talking, and she didn't want to push away the memory of the piquant melody running through her senses, filling her mind and emotions. Music had always had the power to stir her, she reminded herself; but it wasn't just the music. Even with her eyes closed she could see his face smiling intimately into her eyes. As she drifted into sleep with the memory of his fingers rippling over the keyboard, it didn't matter a rap that a million other women might have gazed rapturously at their TV screens, thinking the smile was just for them. For those moments Angela had felt an instant rapport with the man for whom she was going to work. Whether their relationship was going to be smooth or stormy, nothing could change the feelings his music evoked in her.

Chapter Two

Paul telephoned her three days later. Angela had finished her week's notice at the company where she'd worked in public relations, and had done all her packing. The fourth of August was only two days away. Her heart leaped as soon as she recognized his voice on the phone, because it was so unexpected, and she'd already received the details of the departure and the first contact she had to make when they reached Paris.

"There's nothing wrong, is there?" she stammered inanely.

Paul Blake's throaty laugh came across the line.

"Why should anything be wrong just because I phone you, Miss Raines? I merely wanted to suggest that we meet this evening for drinks and a meal, so that we can get to know each other a little better before we leave the country together. I'll pick you up at eight o'clock."

She stared at the mouthpiece of the phone, wishing she had the nerve to tell him to get lost, and ask him why he assumed she was free to accept his invitation, which sounded more like a command? It was typical of his type. She opened her mouth to tell him she had a previous engagement when he forestalled her.

"You haven't got anything fixed up already, have you, Angela?" he spoke softly, and his use of her first name took her by surprise.

"No," she said involuntarily.

"Good. I was about to tell you to cancel it. I'll pick you up at eight."

The line went dead before she could snap furiously that she wasn't used to having her life ordered about, and she was staying in to wash her hair. Let him think she considered that more important than wining and dining with the great Paul Blake! It wasn't, of course. But the way he'd assumed so arrogantly that she'd make no arguments about seeing him irritated her beyond words. If she dared she'd answer the door in her oldest jeans with her hair dripping wet; but if they were going to be in each other's company so much from now on, there was no point in acting so childishly. Presumably that was the way important people behaved, naturally assuming lesser mortals would run around in order to keep them happy.

Angela had washed her hair and showered by the time Lorna came home from her West End office. She was pressing the soft folds of a sea-green dress with a deep-plunging neckline and bell sleeves of which she was especially fond.

"I thought you'd packed that one," Lorna said at once, flopping onto the couch with a sigh of relief.

"I had, but now I'm wearing it tonight——"

"Made up with Tim, have you? I thought he'd come round."

"I'm going out with Paul Blake, if you must know." Angela knew how Lorna would react to that statement, and her friend sat up at once, eyes alight with interest. "And before you read anything into it, he phoned to suggest we get together for a drink and a meal, so we're not complete strangers when we start the tour."

"So there's nothing in it, which is why you're going to wear your sexiest dress for the occasion. Is that it?" Lorna grinned.

Angela looked at it dubiously. Maybe that neckline was too low after all. She caught Lorna's teasing look and shrugged. So what? It would do Mr. Paul Blake good to know he couldn't have everything he saw, no matter how enticing it looked!

And perversely, she made herself look as attractive as she could for the occasion. She told herself it was partly because he'd be used to escorting beautiful women about the town and she didn't want to look like some little country cousin. She told herself she wanted him to be attracted to her, and then she could have the satisfaction of telling him coolly that she wasn't interested. She might even mention Tim as an added deterrent. It would be using him, she thought guiltily; but as he'd never know it, it probably didn't count.

Lorna had left the flat again long before Angela was ready. Lorna's full social life left Angela gasping, but at least it spared her further snide remarks about her appearance, and she admitted that the devil inside her had egged her on. She looked at the finished result in the long bedroom mirror, knowing without false modesty that she'd never looked quite like this before.

The sea-green dress caressed her slim figure, the deep neckline revealing the creamy curves of her breasts seductively. A gold pendant gleamed at her throat, matching the long drop earrings. She had borrowed some of Lorna's makeup—what her flatmate called her "glitter gear"—including cool bronze lipstick and a touch of beige-bronze eye shadow with brown mascara. Her cheekbones were highlighted with just enough color that the overall effect was not too cold; and with her hair a cloud of gold-brown curls, Angie admitted to herself that she looked quite passable. When Paul arrived, and she had opened the door to him with fingers that suddenly seemed all thumbs, his reaction was somewhat different.

He stood inside the door and looked her over deliberately for a full minute without speaking. He unnerved her. She'd overdone it, she thought nervously. He'd thought he was taking on an assistant who was rather intense, devoted to her work and determined to smooth his path for him in the way of all good public relations officers; and what he saw now was a sexpot in green and gold. She forgot all about her intention of trying to give him that impression for the sole purpose of crushing him if needed. She didn't want him to get the *wrong* impression of her. She valued honesty between people above all things—though a swift recollection of the way he'd listened in on her interview with Charlie Cass reminded her that not everyone valued it the way she did. Her stomach settled down a little.

"Well!" He spoke at last, unable to hide the surprise in his voice, or the pleasure. "I hoped this was going to be an interesting evening, but if anybody had told me little Angela Raines could look like a siren I might have doubted them unless I'd seen it for myself. Beauty as well as brains can't be bad!"

It was obviously intended as a compliment, but she wasn't too pleased about being called a siren. Paul looked pretty devastating himself in a dark suede jacket and slacks and a white silk shirt. She found herself thinking that he looked wonderful in dark clothes, with the contrast of white against his tanned skin.

"I didn't know where you were thinking of going this evening, so if what I'm wearing isn't suitable . . ." She was angry with herself for mumbling so inanely, but his long scrutiny was making her jittery.

He moved toward her and put both hands on her slim shoulders. She could feel his strong fingers through the thin fabric of her dress as they brushed gently against her.

"You look wonderful," he said softly. "I'm tempted to suggest we don't go out at all, but I'm not sure I could trust myself. And besides, the showman in me wants to show you off to the rest of London, so maybe we'd better leave."

Angie picked up her bag and followed him woodenly out of the building toward the Aston Martin parked outside. She'd expected a concert pianist to be stuffy and correct, and she'd thought this job would be interesting, if a little cultural, after the textile company she'd just left. But she had the feeling that Paul Blake was the rebel of the classical world. Nothing about him so far added up to her image of the professional musician with wild, untidy hair and a vague expression, such as she'd sometimes seen during symphony concerts when the artist was so completely immersed in the music he was almost on another plane.

She remembered his face on the TV program at that moment. Yes, he shared that much with every other devoted musician, she agreed silently. He was capable of intense feeling . . . she suddenly shivered as she slid into the passenger seat. Joining her, Paul glanced at her enquiringly.

"Are you cold? Shouldn't you have brought a jacket instead of that shawl thing?"

His hands were moving to adjust it around her shoulders and she had to stop herself from jerking away from him.

"I'm quite all right, thank you, Mr. Blake. Just a goose walking over my grave."

He looked at her thoughtfully. *Of course he'd be quite used to having this effect on women,* Angie thought furiously. The adoration, the awe in his presence . . . he'd take it for granted she was nervous at being seen with him. She would have to get used to his arrogance and she'd have to make it plain as quickly as possible that she was no little stage-door groupie ready to gaze at him with stars in her eyes.

"If we're going to be together for the next two months, and hopefully a good deal longer than that, we'd better drop the formality, hadn't we?" he said calmly. "The name's Paul, remember?"

"All right, Paul," she murmured. Using his Christian name shortened the distance between them. She'd been on first-name terms with other employers; even the politician had preferred her to call him Arnold in private, so there was no reason why she should feel anything insidious in Paul Blake's request. But seeing the slight smile on his mouth as she complied, she couldn't help the feeling he was seeing this small victory as the first step toward adding her to his list of conquests.

Well, hard luck, Angie thought. Because she was going to be his first failure.

He drove fast and well in the London traffic, with those strong hands firmly on the wheel. They passed familiar landmarks—Kensington Palace and the Albert Memorial—reminding Angela of the television concert where she had been so moved by Paul's absorption and interpretation of his music. They drove along the leafy coolness of Hyde Park, where couples still strolled about, enjoying the late evening sunshine, past the swish Knightsbridge residences, until they neared the river Thames. Paul steered the car smoothly and expertly into a parking space in the courtyard of an elegant restaurant.

He held her elbow as he led the way inside the plush foyer, and Angela realized she was becoming even more nervous. She couldn't understand why. She'd been in places like this before, and even far more opulent ones. Wining and dining important clients on behalf of the various firms for which she'd worked in public relations had been an integral part of the job. But then it had been more impersonal, she realized instantly. Never on such a one-to-one basis as this job with Paul Blake promised to be.

This discovery led her to think about something that had been niggling away at her for days. Where, for instance, were the hordes of hangers-on one read about following in the train of pop stars and the like? The entourage, the managers, the half-dozen "extras" to underline the importance of the star? Not that she'd expected them to be tagging along on a date, but so far there had been no mention of them. She was curious to know why no one else would be traveling with them on the French tour.

"Why the pensive look?" Paul asked her once they were seated in a window alcove in the lounge bar known as the Tudor Room. The alcove was small and intimate, with red velvet seating and soft warm lighting, even though it was not yet dark, and it had a view of the river that was breathtaking. There were still craft of all sorts plying their way upriver, and the last of the sunlight cast a pinky sheen across the water. Already it looked mysterious and eerie, and as their drinks were served by a waitress dressed in long gown and headdress to complement the Tudor style of the room, Angela could almost imagine the stateliness of a Tudor barge wending its way slowly toward the Tower.

"Hey, come back!" She heard the snap of Paul's fingers beneath her chin, and gave a small laugh. Lorna always told her she was a bit of a nut because she was so susceptible to atmosphere, and would have scolded that she was really going round the bend to imagine Henry's England on a summer night in the twentieth century!

"Sorry! It was a little unexpected to see the river from this angle and this height," she forced herself to say lightly. "It's like a shimmering pink ribbon, isn't it?"

He smiled. "I knew you were the right one for me, despite your little bit of cynicism in Charlie's office. You have a strong romantic streak in you, for all the sophistication. I like women to be feminine the way God intended them to be."

Angela looked at him coolly. It was clearly meant to be a compliment, but he had the most condescending way of saying things that somehow diminished their sincerity.

"I'm sure you'll find me satisfactory——" she began.

"Oh, I'm sure I shall." He was grinning openly at her as the prim words tripped out, his eyes missing nothing of the way a little pulse beat rapidly in her throat. His gaze followed the length of her smooth skin as it was molded by the sea-green of the dress. For a second

32

Angela felt like throwing her arms round her body defensively, and told herself that she was being idiotic to react in this way. He was blatantly, aggressively masculine, and she wasn't the type to twitter in his presence like some lovelorn schoolgirl, even if that was what he expected. She'd handled awkward clients in her time, putting them down so gently and subtly that they never realized it had happened. Somehow she guessed that Paul would need more outspoken rebuffs for the idea to get through to him that she just wasn't interested.

"I expected other people to be accompanying us on the tour." She ignored the implications of his remark and spoke pointedly.

"When you get to know me a little better you'll know why the trade calls me a rebel, Angela. I prefer to call myself a loner—which is why it was so important for me to find the right person to replace Margaret when she up and married her oilman. I don't conform to the practice of taking a truckload of people around with me and paying them for doing the things I can do myself. I don't normally perform with an orchestra, though sometimes I do agree to such a concert; but I'm not formally attached to any big concern. I take the engagements that appeal to me and refuse to become part of any circuit. Charlie Cass sometimes despairs of me, but I don't hear him complaining about the box-office results."

All the time he was speaking, Angela was aware of a tension inside her. She'd already formed the opinion that Paul was arrogant, conceited, sure of himself. And Charlie Cass had already told her they'd be traveling together, so there was no question of her being hired under false pretenses; but another little snippet of the agent's conversation kept running through her mind.

Paul liked a pretty P.R.O. because it kept the stage-door girls away, and if there was a hint of a romance with her, it might help to keep them at bay.

The man was even more egotistical than she'd imagined! Maybe even this dinner tonight was designed as a forerunner to the French tour. At any minute a newspaper photographer might pop up from behind a table and their photos would be emblazoned all over tomorrow's gossip pages. She was letting her imagination run riot and she knew it, but she couldn't rid herself of her contempt for the arrogant Paul Blake. There was a lot to despise in the man, she told herself, despite the fact that he could play the piano like a dream.

His eyes challenged hers across the softly lit table.

"Does it make any difference that you'll be traveling with just your employer instead of with a dozen other people, Angela?"

He looked at her unwaveringly to see her reaction. Her eyes were soft and luminous, the glitter of the gold eye shadow enhancing them, her mouth parted and soft beneath the ridiculous tilted nose that gave her a piquant beauty. That nose intrigued him. She was the girl next door and the seductive sex kitten at one and the same time. It amused him to get her going, to see the sudden flash in those beautiful hazel eyes and the coolness in the fine-arched brows.

She felt a tremor run through her at his gaze. *Oh yes, there is a difference,* she was thinking. A great difference, and he knew it. It all depended on the two persons concerned, of course, but she had a sixth sense that the chemistry between them was going to involve some explosive situations. She forced herself not to glare at the smile spreading across that wide, sensual mouth of his, and resisted the urge to pull her hand away petulantly when his own reached across the table and caught her palm in his sensitive fingers, teasing her.

"I don't think it will cause the slightest problem." She hoped her voice didn't betray the jangling of her nerves. His caressing touch was unspeakably pleasurable, and because she was determined not to be affected by it, her words came out far less than subtle. "I'm not sure what my fiancé thinks about it, though——"

Angie felt the tightening of his fingers on her hand before he released it. There was a sudden coldness in his eyes. *For goodness' sake,* she thought, half amused, *did he think there had never been a man in her life?* But she had to admit it was the devil inside her that had made her refer to Tim as her fiancé, when she'd spent the last few months avoiding that very status.

"I understood you to have no commitments," Paul said angrily.

"Does it bother you?" The little demon was still there, putting a provocative gleam in her eyes. But it seemed Paul's anger was not on account of her being romantically attached at all.

"Yes, it does bother me! This tour is by way of being a trial period on both sides, as you know, but if there's some fiancé waiting in the wings to carry you off, you're going to be no good at all to me, Miss Raines. I need someone always available, so that if an attractive offer is made for me to go to Timbuktu tomorrow, I've every confidence in knowing my P.R.O. will go with me, not start making excuses because of a lovesick boy back home!"

Angela gasped at his arrogance. All he cared about was himself. Charlie needn't worry, she thought furiously. No little stage-door girl was going to lure the magnificent Paul Blake away from his chosen career. He was too much in love with himself to stray off the beaten path, and the girl who married him would always be second best to that colossal ego of his.

"Tim is not a lovesick boy," she said tightly. "But you needn't worry. I'm not thinking of marriage for years yet. I'm quite ready to go to the moon with you if that's what you want!"

He studied her flushed face for a moment, thinking that she was neither the girl next door nor a sex kitten at that instant. She was all woman, beautiful and

35

desirable and defensive, and he felt a sudden urge to break down all those defenses, to hear that melodious voice soften again. Her perfume drifted across the table, tantalizing and fragrant. Paul felt his senses stir. It was against his nature to tread carefully. Other women had told him it was part of his charm, but he knew he had to be cautious with this one. It took some of the fire out of him, knowing he might lose her, and he wanted her as his new assistant. He wanted her very much. She was all that Margaret had been, and more. . . .

"Someday I'll take you there," he said gravely. "Meanwhile, I apologize. It took me by surprise, that's all. Coupled with the fact that you don't wear an engagement ring."

Angie's glance went automatically to her left hand. Stupid of her. Of course he wouldn't miss that. She was taken aback by his apology and the sudden change of mood. And the lyrical reply to her sarcastic comment about going to the moon!

She spoke hurriedly. "It's not official yet."

Paul's face broke into one of his illuminating smiles that made her catch her breath.

"Good. Engagements are made to be broken, and engagements that aren't even official can be disregarded, can't they?"

"I wouldn't say that." Angela felt the prickles start at the back of her neck. He had the power to antagonize her more quickly than any man she had ever met. "Tim and I have a very special relationship. He means a good deal to me, and I don't anticipate having to lose touch with all my old friends just because I take on a new job." Her voice was sharp and touchy.

Paul's jaw had squared as she started talking, especially when she called her relationship with Tim very special. But the sardonic expression was back in his eyes again now.

"If I was practically engaged to you, my lovely

Angela, I would clinch it very quickly. You wouldn't go taking any new job that took you away from me for two months!"

The man was impossible. She had expected some kind of temperament. In an artist it was understandable, even forgivable to a certain degree; but to begin commenting on such personal matters on such short acquaintance was practically insulting. No doubt he thought it flattering, she thought witheringly. No doubt plenty of other women had fallen for his brash masculinity and the way he oozed sex appeal.

Angela hadn't missed the way several groups of people had glanced their way, obviously recognizing Paul. And the glances that came from women were usually met by a brief smile on his part. A smile that said, "I know I'm attractive and I know you recognize me, so here's a crumb of a smile."

The Tudor waitress arrived with their meal, saving Angela the trouble of searching for a reply. Paul had ordered a bottle of Anjou rosé wine to accompany the steaks and salad, and the food and drink were wonderful. Angela felt herself slowly relaxing as her companion moved the conversation away from personal topics and spoke a little about the tour.

"The itinerary begins in Paris. Have you been there before, Angela?"

"No."

"Then you're in for a treat. Everyone should go to Paris. It's a city made for lovers." He couldn't resist that, of course.

"I must tell Tim," Angela said lightly, and had the satisfaction of catching a small scowl on his handsome face. He hated to have another man flaunted at him when he was in the mood for teasing, she realized. It was a little card to keep up her sleeve.

"How long are we in Paris?" she asked hurriedly, reminding herself that if she irritated him too much he might just tell her to get lost and find someone else to act as his P.R.O. And however much she despised the kind of man he was, she wanted this job. Besides, he intrigued her. She couldn't deny it.

"About ten days. I want to take a couple of days to relax after my last tour, which was pretty strenuous, and then there will be a few press meetings and so on; and there's talk of a French record company wanting to do a set of LPs, so there will be discussions on that. Charlie will be sending you all the info before we leave. I shall want several days for rehearsals and then there are three evening concerts at the Théatre des Fleurs."

"Theater of flowers," Angela murmured. "Sounds nice."

"It is. There's a tradition attached to it too. Whatever time of year it is, the theater is decorated with the appropriate flowers. It can be quite heady in summer when the hall is filled with the scent of roses. We shall probably be just in time for them. Autumn is perhaps the best time to perform if you suffer from hayfever, when they have the most marvelous displays of chrysanthemums and autumn leaves——" He paused as she began laughing softly. "Have I said something funny?"

Angela's mind had winged back instantly to the Albert Hall concert, when she had sat so entranced in front of her TV set, watching those strong, sensitive fingers manipulate the piano keys. It had been pure magic to listen to the music, and to see the involvement on his handsome features. She felt a wild thrill run through her involuntarily, and a sudden confusion made her tongue-tied.

"I heard you play that piece at the Albert Hall concert that was televised." She knew she was flustered as he looked at her enquiringly. "'Autumn Leaves' . . . it has always been one of my favorites and I—I thought it was wonderful."

The smile spread slowly across his face, starting at his mouth and enlivening his eyes. The little frown lines she'd noticed between them on the TV screen as he concentrated on a serious piece of music were completely gone for the moment, and instead the little laughter lines fanned out from the corners of those velvet brown eyes. Angela felt the warmth of his personality reach out toward her, and instantly she knew how the front-row ladies must feel at one of his concerts when he turned and smiled at them. As if the smile was for one person alone. . . . And she guessed too how it must feel when Paul threw the red rose from his buttonhole, as he did sometimes, and one of them caught it to keep as a memento. Angela, who could never resist keepsakes herself, suddenly felt the full power of his magnetic charm as it turned on her.

It was hard to regain her composure, but she knew she had to steer the conversation to a less personal level.

"I was interested in your choice of the piece, as a matter of fact." She hoped her voice gave no indication of the way her heart was hammering. "It's so much less formal than the usual repertoire of a concert pianist."

"Surely you wouldn't deny that modern composers can produce music just as important as that of Mozart, for instance?" Paul said at once. "People tend to forget that all composers are contemporary in their day, so why not honor them while they're still around, if they deserve it? And most audiences are pleased by a variety of pieces. A solid program of chamber music can be just as wearing as an evening of jazz."

"Don't let my flatmate hear you say that." Angela grinned. "Lorna is a jazz fanatic."

"Really? And how about you?"

"I like all kinds of music," Angela replied, thinking ruefully that the topic had come neatly back to her opinion again. "Though I confess I find classical music more stimulating than any other kind, and a modern composition given the classical treatment the way you do it with 'Autumn Leaves' is especially exciting, though I suppose the purists would argue with that."

"Would you like a private performance after we leave here?" Paul said. "My house is only half an hour's drive away, and we could have coffee and a nightcap there, Angela. Unless you're afraid to be in such intimate surroundings with me, of course."

His voice was slightly mocking, and all the tension was back between them again in an instant. Angela was angry at the way he could change the mood so subtly, and angry too at the way her heart had leaped at the intense look in his eyes.

Oh, but he knows exactly the effect he has on women! she thought. He fully expected her to fall into his arms just because he'd lifted his little finger toward her—or act like some Victorian maiden and twitter like an idiot as she declined his invitation!

"Naturally, I'd be honored, if you really mean it," she replied coolly, her voice steady, her eyes revealing nothing. "It's not every day I get such an offer from a star, and Lorna will be even more intrigued when I tell her. She can't quite understand how anyone can get so enthusiastic about classical music. And what's more, she'll be dying to know if a concert pianist can be as human as the rest of us lesser mortals. I'm sure she thinks of you as a race apart."

She didn't mean to decry Lorna at all by her flippant remarks. If anything, she knew she was being deliberately provoking to Paul, and that his ego wouldn't take too kindly to such suggestions. Angela knew she was right when he attacked his steak with renewed vigor.

"I assure you I can be very human, Angela, and I wouldn't dream of keeping Cinderella out too late, though it may well be after midnight. You'll be delivered home in one piece, don't worry."

Angela guessed he wasn't too keen on the thought of her reporting everything to Lorna. Not that she had any intention of doing so, but it wouldn't hurt Paul to think so. His ego could do with being pruned a little.

When they left the restaurant the night was filled

with a soft darkness, and the winding river was still and glassy, the moonlight streaking it with silver. Paul drove without speaking, and Angie wondered if he was regretting his suggestion to play for her. Maybe she wasn't reacting in exactly the way he was used to; but if she was to work for him, it was the only way possible, she reasoned. It would be fatal to fall in love with him.

The Aston Martin stopped outside an elegant mews house on a small cobbled street that was a quaint feature of London's hidden charms. The street was lit by mellow lighting in old-fashioned lamp standards, and they might have been transported back a hundred years but for the few smart cars standing outside the opulent houses. Paul led the way and opened the front door for her. She realized her legs were feeling like jelly, and put it down to the wine, but she knew that wasn't the only cause.

It was a beautiful house. Everything was deep-pile carpeted, and the furniture was made of velvet and leather. In one corner of the lounge a stately grand piano stood, with wall lighting directed at the keyboard and music stand. Angela's eyes were drawn at once to the photographs on a side table. Some were of Paul at various concerts or winning awards, some of other people. She'd never thought of him as a family man, but there was an older couple, obviously his parents, and several of an attractive woman with coal-black hair and a smoldering sexuality in her expression as she smiled at the camera. Paul caught the look on Angela's face as she looked at it and he picked it up smilingly.

"Beautiful, isn't she?"

"Is she your wife?" The words were out before Angela could stop them. Why shouldn't he have a wife? The thought deflated her for some reason. She couldn't be *here*. . . .

Paul laughed. "I haven't been caught in that trap yet, my lovely Angela! Don't you recognize her? She would be most annoyed to hear that, though I admit she's not

41

as well known in this country as in France. She's Claudette Dubois."

Angela still looked vague. The name meant nothing to her, not even when Paul told her Claudette was one of France's darlings, and a stunning opera singer. She smiled politely. He must know plenty of beautiful women, and more than one must have wanted to catch him in that trap, as he put it. She felt suddenly out of her depth in this lovely house, among the trappings of a successful artist. Her previous appointments as a P.R.O. had been among staid businessmen and a politician who had had a wife to front all the important social occasions, while Angela stayed discreetly in the background seeing that all ran smoothly.

Somehow she felt she was going to be well in the foreground in Paul's employ. To ward off the groupies . . . she could almost hear Charlie Cass reminding her. Practically acting the part of a wife, with all the responsibilities and none of the advantages. Angela felt her face flood with color as she realized she had been staring hard and long at the photo of Claudette Dubois, and that Paul was taking it gently from her hands.

"I daresay you'll get the chance to meet her," he said carelessly. Her heart jolted, for no sensible reason.

"Did you mention coffee?" she said jerkily. "I told you I didn't want to be late home——"

Paul picked up an internal phone and asked someone called Mrs. Edwards to bring coffee for two to the lounge in fifteen minutes. *This is how the other half lives,* Angie thought. She realized she was very much on edge, as if expecting the great seduction scene at any minute, and reminding herself not to be so stupid, because presumably there was a housekeeper called Mrs. Edwards brewing coffee for them at this very moment.

"Why don't you relax, Angela, and I'll give you what you came for?" he said softly.

She perched on the edge of a velvet armchair, but instead of suggesting she try the sofa he gave a short laugh and moved away from her to the piano. From her chair she had a side view of his strong profile, and the mobility of his hands as they flowed over the keyboard. She relaxed with a little sigh of pleasure as the haunting melody of "Clair de Lune" filled the room. Paul's touch was exquisite, one moment rippling delicately over the keys, the next exploding rapturously as the music ended.

Did he expect her to applaud, Angie wondered, as the piece faded into silence? She did nothing, all her attention focused on those mobile fingers and the changing expressions on his face as he lived out the music in his head. Sometimes he seemed to be obsessed with the melody to the exclusion of all else; at other times he looked toward Angie with a half smile on his lips, or an unfathomable look in his eyes.

Paul played several short pieces, and then, predictably, his own arrangement of "Autumn Leaves." This was the classical version he'd played during the television concert. The music lent itself beautifully to the formal treatment he gave it, but even while Angie was totally absorbed in its magic, the tempo changed. It was still the same music, but now Paul slowed it down to a seductively slow, intimate contemporary version.

His eyes were watching her, and Angie felt the breath catch in her throat as a warm color began to suffuse her neck and cheeks. Her heart beat rapidly, and a feeling almost akin to despair ran through her, as if she was rushing headlong into something from which there was no escape. She couldn't look away from Paul's intense gaze. The music stopped so abruptly it made her gasp.

Angela ran her tongue around her dry lips, suddenly nervous. Earlier, the maid had unobtrusively brought in a tray with two cups and a percolator of coffee, and

Angela gestured toward it. Paul arose from the piano and moved slowly toward her with all the deliberation of a tiger stalking its prey.

"Would you like me to pour the coffee?" she spoke too quickly, giving herself away, and she saw the hint of a smile touch his mouth.

"No," he said in a soft voice. "The coffee can wait."

"I thought that was what we came here for——" she tried to remain brisk, but it was impossible.

Even when he wasn't touching her, she was terribly aware of the man and fascinated by him. If she was the fanciful sort, she would have said he was seducing her by the sheer force of his personality and the enchantment of his music, and she realized only too well what a mistake it had been to come to his home with him. As he reached her, the fresh tang of his cologne tingled in her nostrils, evocative and sensual.

She seemed helpless as Paul drew her into his arms. He touched his lips to hers with little ghost kisses that inflamed her senses, leaving her breathless, and wanting more. She barely managed to remain in control of her own emotions, and kept reminding herself that it would be fatal to plunge into a romantic affair with Paul Blake. They were to be in such close contact over the next two months, it was vital that their relationship should be platonic. At least, it was vital to Angie's peace of mind.

"I've been wanting to kiss you ever since I felt those sparks flying between us in Charlie's office." Paul was speaking softly against her mouth now. "I hope you believe in Kismet as much as I do, sweet Angela."

Oh, it was unfair, Angie thought weakly, as his hands traveled slowly over the contours of her back as if to imprint the shape of her on his memory forever. Her knees felt suddenly shaky, and without thinking she leaned against him more heavily. She could feel the beating of his heart, as wild and erratic as her own.

She hardly knew how it was happening, but somehow

he was propelling her toward the settee, and as her calves touched it she was sinking onto its softness, with Paul's arms still around her.

"Paul, please——" she protested weakly as he drew her to him again, his lips seeking hers more passionately.

He paused for a moment with his lips a breath away from her, his face darkly above her, and almost to her own despair, she knew she didn't want him to pause. She swallowed thickly at the realization of how dangerously vulnerable she was after all.

"You aren't going to give out with some ridiculous outdated morals, are you, Angie?" Paul said softly. "The days when a red-blooded man wasn't expected to kiss a desirable young woman until the wedding day are long since gone, thank God! There's nothing wrong in admitting a mutual attraction."

Nothing wrong, as long as that was as far as it went. Angie knew instinctively that Paul wasn't the kind of man to be satisfied with a few chaste kisses, and she didn't want to be added to his list of conquests. She wouldn't admit, either, that something very basic in her own nature cried out for his kisses; but the knowledge made her even more determined to be the one that got away.

"Do you always treat your assistants to a glimpse of your masterful technique as soon as they're hired?" She tried to sound as if she was amused, but totally unaffected by him. "Is this the way you count on their loyalty, by the personal Paul Blake touch? I hadn't realized *quite* how personal your personal assistant was expected to be!"

It was guaranteed to make him angry and she knew it. She saw the flash in his eyes, and guessed he wasn't used to having his advances treated so casually. The next minute she felt his fingertip beneath her chin, and she was forced to look directly into his magnetic brown eyes.

"Are you trying to minimize the attraction between us, Angie?" He was aggressively masculine now, the softness gone. "Or kidding yourself that it doesn't exist at all?"

His eyes dared her to deny it as his finger traced the curve of her throat beneath her chin. She couldn't restrain a dry swallow. Of course it existed! It was stronger than anything she'd ever known before, which was why it scared her so. It was too sudden, too overpowering . . . too much everything she'd known was lacking in her feelings for Tim. The fleeting thought of Tim brought his image to the forefront of her mind. She twisted her face away from Paul's caressing finger and his demanding, hypnotic gaze.

"I don't pretend it doesn't exist," she said deliberately. "But that doesn't mean I intend to do anything about it. And it certainly doesn't mean I'm going to fall eagerly into your arms every time we're alone! I already have a boyfriend. Remember?"

In the small silence that followed her remarks, Angie was conscious of the pulse beating wildly in her throat. She prayed that Paul couldn't read her mind at that moment. If he'd done so, he'd surely have guessed how badly she wanted him to pull her into his arms again with that rough aggressiveness that both shocked and excited her. She was stunned at the force of her own reactions, and she felt both relieved and disappointed when Paul gave a short laugh and let her go.

"I don't think he's that important to you, my sweet." There was an edge to his voice now. "And I guarantee you won't be reminding me of his existence once we get to know each other better. As for my choice of personal assistant—as you should be perceptive enough to know —it's essential for me to have someone with whom I'm in complete accord. My temperament demands a smooth uncomplicated relationship with my assistant. I trust that's how it will be for us, Angela."

He left her on the settee while he strode across the

room to pour the coffee. She felt a little as if she'd been reprimanded like a naughty schoolgirl. It was ridiculous, since he'd been the one to get out of line, she told herself angrily. Now he was going all starchy on her because she'd mentioned Tim at such an inopportune moment and ruffled his artistic sensitivity. Well, it was his hard luck. She could be ruffled too, and if she had to use Tim to keep Paul at arm's length, then use him she would.

She felt guilty even as the idea spun into her mind. She'd been fond of Tim for a long time, and the thought of using him in any way wasn't a very comfortable one. She felt guilty too at the knowledge that part of her didn't want to keep Paul at arm's length at all, and in her most honest moments she admitted to herself that he was the most exciting man she'd ever met.

How could she deny it, when every glance between them provoked a shower of sparks in her head? When every brush of his hand was enough to set her senses tingling. When the memory of those tantalizing little kisses stayed with her long into the night after he drove her home?

She had done the most reckless thing in the world by accepting this job as Paul's personal assistant. But to change her mind now would be as impossible as asking the sun not to follow the rain. For better or worse, she had committed herself. As Angie drifted into sleep that night, those were the words that merged with the image of Paul's face and the memory of his kisses. For better or worse . . . she turned restlessly beneath the bedcovers and buried her face in the pillow, willing sleep to come, and trying not to think of him.

Chapter Three

Tim insisted on seeing her off at the airport, though she assured him it wasn't necessary, and felt acutely embarrassed at the thought of the two men eyeing each other aggressively. Charlie Cass was also there with last-minute good wishes, so it was an unlikely foursome waiting for the call to board the plane at Heathrow.

"You'll write now and then to let me know how you are, I suppose?" Tim still hadn't forgiven her for making her rejection of him final, and his voice was petulant as it so often was. Angela had never realized it before, or maybe she just hadn't been looking for faults when she'd thought she and Tim might have a future together.

"Of course I shall," she spoke warmly. He'd been part of her life for too long for her to want to leave him on bad terms. Impulsively she hugged him, wishing they'd just been able to walk right on board. These lengthy goodbyes did no one any good, and she didn't miss the cold way Paul was looking at her. She'd told him she and Tim were practically engaged, she remembered, and to reinforce her statement she pressed a fervent kiss on his lips when their call finally came.

"Have a good trip, Angie," he whispered huskily in her ear. "Maybe when you get back——"

"I won't change my mind, Tim," she whispered back. "But I'll always love you as a friend. You know that, and I value your friendship, so don't take it away from me."

He hugged her closer in answer. To the others it must have looked like a lovers' embrace—and so much the better, Angie thought defiantly as she and Paul walked toward Passport Control. The other night had unnerved her badly. It had been a mistake to go back to Paul's house alone with him, as he could affect her so much without even touching her. She was under no illusions now about his effect on women. She admitted, but only to herself, that there had been moments when a fire had been raging inside her. She must be mad to undertake this tour with him, but she knew too that nothing would stop her. She was determined to prove to herself that she was strong enough to resist his blatant brand of sexuality.

"That was a very touching little scene," he commented coldly once they had found their seats on the plane. He allowed her the window seat, and she was suddenly conscious of a dryness in her throat as she took it automatically. She hated flying, but the past days had been so busy and hectic she'd hardly thought about it until this minute. She turned to retort to her companion, but felt a sudden dizziness wash over her as the stewardesses began their routine of explaining the seat-belt procedure and demonstrating the use of oxygen masks and life belts.

Paul took one look at her white face, in which her hazel eyes appeared enormous, and ordered her to put her head on her knees. Never had she felt so foolish, but she was too queasy to resist. She vaguely heard him speak to a stewardess, and the next minute Paul pulled her gently back in the seat and handed her a glass of water and a pill, which she swallowed obediently. They hadn't even left the ground yet, and she felt as if every eye was looking at her.

"I'm terribly sorry," she mumbled. "I didn't have time for any breakfast this morning, and the thought of flying just got to me."

"For a minute I thought we were going to have to

leave you behind. You'll be fine once we're airborne and the lunch comes round. They provide food right away especially for dimwits like you, you know."

He might have been saying it just to calm her or it might be true, she didn't know. She closed her eyes as the engines revved up, rigid in her seat, and then she felt Paul's hand take hold of her own. She made no attempt to pull it away. She was glad of its reassuring warmth, and her fingers curled tightly round his. It would be all right once they leveled out and the seat-belt lights went off, she reminded herself. She was always able to relax a little when the plane was in the air.

The meal saved Angela the embarrassment of trying to find conversation after their little clash. Afterward she concentrated on trying to read a paperback, but in no time, it seemed, Paul told her that they were approaching Paris. Angela looked out the window, stilling the sudden anxiety about landing inside her. They had to come down, for goodness' sake; and once there, she could stay on solid ground for a couple of months. He pointed out the curving arc of the Seine as it meandered through the countryside. The sky was particularly clear, and as he leaned over her, she followed the direction of his pointing finger to see the faint outline of the Eiffel Tower and the city's tallest buildings in the distance.

Angela ignored the closeness of her companion, knowing instinctively that he was deliberately provoking her. His cheeks brushed against hers and his thigh pressed against her leg as he lifted back the armrest between them. She would not let him know it affected her in the slightest.

There was a new excitement flooding her veins that had nothing to do with Paul Blake, she insisted to herself. It was the delight of being about to see Paris, with all the familiar scenes she'd only read about coming to life in front of her.

Paul was obliged to replace the armrest as the seat-belt sign went on again and the announcement was made that they would soon be coming in to land. Angela breathed a small sigh of relief. She didn't argue as his hand reached for hers again during the approach, but she let it lie limply against her own and kept her eyes firmly closed until she felt the bump of the tires on the ground.

At that moment Paul leaned across and kissed her.

"Ten out of ten for control," he said lightly, "in all respects, dear Angela!" Before she could respond sarcastically, he leaned forward again and kissed the tip of her nose. "Do you know you've got the most ridiculous nose I've ever seen?"

He was standing up and reaching for their coats from the overhead compartment while she raged at his cheek. Lorna and Tim and quite a few others in the past had referred to it as cute and endearing, but Angela had always been painfully aware of its imperfection, and hated any reference to it. That Paul should make such a comment about it when she was at her most vulnerable at the end of a harrowing plane journey stamped him as insufferably rude.

"Did your previous assistant enjoy your personal observations?" she said stiffly. She shrugged her arms into her light jacket, resisting any help from him by twisting away from his hands.

"She wasn't as touchy as you seem to be," he retorted. "I'm going to miss her."

He strode up the emptying aisle of the plane, leaving her to follow with her own hand baggage. The sting of furious tears misted her eyes for a moment. *She* was touchy! His Margaret must have been a saint to have kept her job with him for so long, Angela thought savagely.

She caught up with him at the doorway. He stood tall and elegant, and she guessed from the way the stewardesses were smiling up at him that he was revealing his most charming self for their benefit. Of course he would. He was a star, wasn't he?

Once they reached the reception lounge, Angela realized how true that was. A small group of people surged forward at Paul's arrival, and several newspaper photographers asked him to pause a moment while they took a few shots.

"Smile, Angela," he breathed at her through his smile. "Part of your job is to provide the female interest for the newshounds! Try to look as if you're enjoying it, there's a love."

He tucked her arm in his, his hand caressing her arm through the thin material of her suit. There wasn't a thing she could do about it as several reporters gabbled away in rapid French at Paul. She was fluent enough to understand the enquiries about his lovely companion, and his own laughing replies that they'd have to wait and see. She was outraged. Why didn't he merely tell the truth, that she was here as his assistant and nothing else? From the arch replies he was giving them, they were going to put a very different interpretation on their appearance together.

"Come on, let's get out of here," he said suddenly. "They'll have us cornered all day if we're not careful, and Charlie will have arranged the usual hired car to be waiting for us. Once we're at the hotel we can relax a bit and I can safely leave the rest of the business problems to you, can't I, my sweet?"

His words were plain and simple, spoken in English close to her ear, but to the waiting reporters it must have seemed like a very intimate little moment as he squeezed her arm and brushed her cheek with his lips—a moment that wasn't missed by the expectant cameras. Paul led the way to the entrance, after waving the reporters aside with an imperious hand. There was an airport employee waiting by a white car outside the Orly entrance, and he tipped his hand to his forehead as soon as he saw Paul. Obviously it was a routine that had been followed before.

"I thought you'd have had a chauffeur," Angela said shortly as the luggage was piled in the back seat.

"I prefer the freedom of driving myself. Despite the traffic, I find driving relaxes me. Besides, when we have a good many places to visit on tour, it means I can please myself about when and where I stop, provided we stay on schedule."

Angela felt an odd little shiver run through her. His words were innocuous enough, but she had the strangest feeling about this entire journey. It was as if she and this man she hardly knew were driving off into the sunset, to wherever his whims took him. It was true that she hardly knew him, she realized, and yet in some ways she knew him better than she had known any man before, even Tim. There was an empathy between them that she couldn't deny, sometimes making her feel unbearably close to him, sometimes making her rage against him.

She forced herself to realize the sense of his comment about driving himself as he slid behind the wheel and steered the car out onto the right-hand side of the road in the continental manner, and headed north, toward the city. There were many cities to visit after Paris . . . Orléans, Nantes, Bordeaux, Lyons, Cannes, Marseilles. The names ran through Angela's head with the ease of a child's recitation, and as always the thrill of seeing new places accompanied them.

The car mingled in the rushing traffic of Paris. Paul was obliged to give every bit of his concentration to his driving, just managing to comment briefly on each new part of the city that came into view. Dominating all of course, to her delight, was the fairylike structure of the Eiffel Tower, deceptively fragile looking in its iron tracery.

"Beautiful, isn't it?" Paul said, as she commented on

it. "I suppose you know it was Gustave Eiffel who designed the interior of the Statue of Liberty in New York too?"

"I think I remember hearing it somewhere," Angie nodded. "That's somewhere else I plan to visit someday."

"I'll see if it can be arranged," Paul said sardonically.

She ignored him. She was too excited at actually being in Paris to care about his snide remarks. The thrill of seeing it all was acute. It was exactly as Angela had pictured it, with its wide tree-lined avenues and elegant boulevards. Yet no travel brochure could portray the indefinable atmosphere of Paris. There was an excitement in the air that was essentially Paris. Angie asked Paul how far it was to their hotel. She wouldn't have minded riding round and round the city all day.

"It's right in the heart of the city," he said abruptly, and she could tell he didn't echo her sentiments as cars seemed to hurl themselves in their direction with maniacal near misses. "I trust it will all be to your satisfaction when we arrive."

She sensed that he was as tense as she was, in their close proximity, and the thought gave her a small feeling of relief. It made him slightly vulnerable too, and not quite as confident as he'd have her believe. Remembering that her job was supposed to be to smooth his path for him and that he was a noted artist, she made no retaliatory remark. Instead, she let her eyes feast on the splendors of the medieval and eighteenth-century architecture, and the occasional glimpses of the gray-green river Seine.

"It's like another world to me," she said breathlessly.

A world made for lovers, she thought. Wasn't that what the poets said of Paris? Angie realized how many of the people strolling about the streets were couples, wandering arm-in-arm, as if just being here was all they needed to trigger the feeling of *amour.* The air was fragrant with blossoming romance, and the chic young women and attentive young men made her suddenly long for someone of her own to love.

"We're nearing the Champs Élysées," Paul's abrupt voice told her. "It was once a patch of marshland outside the heart of the city, until a couple of centuries ago. It's hard to imagine it now, isn't it?"

"It's fantastic," Angie breathed. All of Paris seemed to converge on the fashionable street of shops and cinemas and street cafes with their tables and chairs outside on the pavements, decked with brightly-colored umbrellas. From this wide avenue, Parisians and tourists alike watched the world go by.

Ahead of them now was the magnificent Arc de Triomphe.

"I've no idea of the history of it," Angie commented. "I feel I should have done my homework before coming here, but there wasn't much time——"

Paul was forced to stop the car in the crush of traffic. He gave a brief smile as she craned her neck to see the beautiful curved arch above them. The approach along the tree-lined avenue had been impressive enough. Now, Angie was staggered at the size of the monument.

"Basically, it's a tribute to Napoleon," Paul informed her. "His hearse passed beneath the arch on its return from St. Helena in 1840. There are a hundred stone pillars round the arch, said to represent the hundred days——"

He stopped speaking as the traffic started to flow again, and their car moved forward. Angie looked at him with new respect.

"I hadn't realized you were so knowledgeable about it——"

"Did you assume a pianist knows nothing but crochets and quavers, Angela?"

"Of course not." He was putting her on the defensive again.

"I've spent a lot of time in Paris," he commented, reminding her of the photo of the glamorous lady at his house, Claudette something-or-other. She turned back for another look at the Arc de Triomphe as he went on speaking. "A perpetual flame burns beneath the arch by the tomb of an unknown soldier of the First World War. It's an impressive piece of architecture, but personally I find it a bit depressing with all its morbid connections."

She was learning more about Paul all the time, Angela realized. She should have known that an artistic temperament would be receptive to the atmosphere surrounding the sad as well as the beautiful. For most visitors to Paris, the Arc de Triomphe was merely one more item on the sight-seeing agenda. The Paul Blakes of this world would see something far deeper.

As they drove alongside the waters of the Seine once more, the sun glinted like diamonds on its rippling surface. The river was dotted with craft of every description, from working boats to glass-topped pleasure boats, the famous *bateaux mouches*. Alongside the river the glossy leaves of the horse-chestnut trees waved in the gentle breeze. These images of Paris were fast making her fall in love with this city of grace and love.

"It's beautiful," she said involuntarily. Paul glanced at her rapt face and smiled.

"It's always more beautiful seeing it through someone else's eyes to whom it's all new and fresh. We'll have time for some proper sight-seeing later on, but I think we'll leave the car safely at the hotel and take the Métro. You might as well soak up as many of the sights as you can. I warn you I'm likely to become intolerable by the end of the week."

Angela nearly laughed out loud. Clearly he had no idea that he had already irritated her beyond words on several occasions, or that she found his arrogance unbearable at times, or that she could melt into unbelievable pleasure when his music filled her senses. Perhaps he had a little idea about *that*, she thought

56

hurriedly. Of his effect on women, she had no doubt he was very much aware and played up to it to the nth degree.

The hotel where they were staying was one of the best in Paris. Opulent and ornately grand, it was decorated by huge crystal chandeliers in the foyer and palm trees seeming to grow out of the thick pile carpets. A flunky appeared at once to attend to the luggage, and seconds later a male voice called to Paul from the recesses of one of the many leather couches.

"Paul, here you are at last. I refrained from joining the crush at the airport, guessing this would be your destination. Come and join me for a drink and give me a private interview!"

Angela heard Paul laugh as the other man rose to greet him. He was shorter than Paul, fair-haired and extremely elegant, wearing a tweed jacket, casual slacks, a black silk shirt undone to the waist and a carelessly knotted cravat at his throat. He spoke perfect English, but Angela suspected immediately that he wasn't British.

Paul turned swiftly toward her. "Perhaps you would begin your public relating in a moment, Angela." He indicated the desk. "And then please do come and meet Jacques."

She felt as if she'd been dismissed as he turned away, but she had noticed the way the other man had eyed her curiously. How many other so-called "assistants" had Paul brought on his tours when the efficient Margaret hadn't been available, she wondered? It was no concern of hers, and she went to the desk and spoke in rapid French, signing for both of them and receiving two enormous gilt keys to their rooms. The luggage disappeared into the lift after the bellboy ascertained the appropriate rooms, and Angela had no choice but to join the two men.

They both jumped up as she approached, and she sat down awkwardly between them, since they automatically separated for her. Jacques snapped his fingers and a bottle of wine and three glasses appeared as if by magic. No money changed hands. This Jacques evidently had good standing here, though she assumed him to be a reporter from his greeting—a very elegant reporter, however.

"I am enchanted to meet you, Miss Raines." He smiled into her eyes with boyish charm. She could imagine him wheedling an interview out of anyone. "I have told Paul how I envy him his choice of companion——"

"I am his assistant, Monsieur."

"But of course! Won't you introduce us properly, Paul?"

Angela realized Paul was enjoying himself, and the next moment she knew why.

"Certainly. Miss Angela Raines, Comte Jacques Vincennes."

Angela felt her cheeks grow pink as he took her hand and raised it to his lips in the continental manner.

"Oh, forgive me——"

"It is of no matter, my dear Angela, and your confusion suits you. I do not stand on ceremony among friends, and my name is Jacques."

She warmed to him at once. He had an easy air about him that demanded nothing but return friendship. Presumably a French count was quite happy to work as a journalist these days, and as she joined in the conversation, she learned that Jacques intended to follow the progress of Paul's tour.

"My magazine wishes to do a complete profile, Paul," Jacques explained. "And as I have the final say in things, I have decided it would be pleasant to do it myself—and even more pleasant now that I know the delightful Miss Raines will be accompanying us!"

"Angela," she reminded him with a smile. He was no ordinary reporter then! Most likely he owned the magazine he'd mentioned. She was suddenly aware that

Paul's handsome face was frowning a little. Perhaps he thought she was attempting to flirt with his friend, she surmised. The idea appealed to her. Let him think she fancied this French count! It might make him realize there were other men in the world who attracted women besides himself. She smiled even more warmly at Jacques.

"I would be honored if you would both join me for dinner at my club tonight——" Jacques began.

Paul interrupted him brusquely. "Not tonight, Jacques. We're both tired from the flight, but I promised to show Angela a little bit of Paris tonight, and I can't go back on that. I suspect that will be enough for both of us. But maybe tomorrow?"

"Of course," Jacques said at once. But the knowing smile he gave wasn't lost on Angela, and she was indignant at the way Paul had presumed to take her over. She might be working for him, but he didn't own her. It was ridiculous to say they were tired after the short flight from London to Paris. If she didn't know better, she might think he was jealous; but that was ludicrous. Unless it was his ego that couldn't stand the thought of another man intruding into her thoughts.

Jacques rose to leave them, taking her hand and touching it lightly with his lips once more. It was a charming custom, she thought, that made her feel deliciously feminine. Some people could learn a lot about finesse from Comte Jacques Vincennes, she thought scathingly. She watched as he moved easily toward the great glass swinging doors of the hotel and disappeared into the Paris sunshine.

"If you can tear yourself away from your daydreams, it would be a good idea to unpack," Paul's voice called her back.

She looked at him coolly. "He's a very attractive man, isn't he? Does he own the magazine he spoke about?"

"He does. And he's quite rich. He has no need to

work, but he chooses to do so. Anything else you need to know, or will that be enough to whet your appetite for now?"

Angela felt the antagonism rising quickly between them.

"Why do you have to be so offensive to me?" she said quietly. "I didn't know this was part of the job. If you'll excuse me, I'll do as you say and unpack and have a shower. That is permitted, I suppose? Your plans don't exclude such things?"

She went inside her room and slammed the door behind her, knowing it was a childish gesture, but suddenly not caring.

It took a few seconds before she could move across to her luggage and start to unpack. She looked around her room, which was very comfortable with a huge bed, a thickly carpeted floor and an ornately decorated dressing-table. Off to her right was a shower cubicle and bathroom. She gave a small sigh, abandoned the unpacking, and decided to take a cool shower first. She had just taken off all her clothes when there was a tap on the outer door. She threw on a terry bathrobe quickly and went to answer it.

Paul stood there, holding her hand luggage. She moved back automatically, but before she could argue he was inside her room. She felt a flutter of unease mixed with something far more basic as the memory of the way he had held her back in his house and her own responses rose vividly in her mind.

"The bellboy put both pieces of hand luggage in my room," he said abruptly.

"Thank you." She was suddenly tongue-tied, ashamed of the way she had spoken to him earlier, and wishing he hadn't made it necessary.

"I've ordered dinner for seven," he went on in that oddly jerky tone. "I thought we'd have it here, then we can see a bit of the city. Does that suit you?"

"Of course." She felt embarrassed now. "But I'm quite capable of finding my own way about, you know. You don't have to——"

"Wipe your nose? I think that was the inelegant way you termed it in Charlie's office, wasn't it? No, I don't have to do that, Miss Raines, nor do I have to keep you on since we seem to get on each others' nerves so much. But I *want* to keep you on, and I *want* to have dinner with you and show you Paris. And just for the record, when I said your nose was ridiculous, I might also have said it's beautiful and charming and adorable too, but if I had I'm quite sure you'd have suspected my motives. Wouldn't you?"

Angela's face broke into a sudden smile as she admitted that she would have. He stepped forward and put his hands on the shoulders of her bathrobe. She knew he was going to kiss her again, and she still didn't know whether to resist or not by the time he bent his head and touched her mouth lightly with his lips. She could feel the hardness of his body pressed against hers, and a little sigh escaped her lips as the kiss ended, almost as if she had wanted it to go on forever.

"I'd have meant it all the same," Paul said softly. He let his hands run slowly down the length of her arms and she suppressed a small shiver. "Be ready at six forty-five. I'll call for you."

He told her she looked stunning the moment he saw her. The black dress was chic enough for dinner, threaded with metallic silver that shimmered in the bodice and sleeves. The skirt was plain and swirling, and her legs were encased in sheer black silk and high-heeled sandals. For their sight-seeing evening, she took a honey-colored stole in case it got cooler later. She knew she looked her best, and a little glow went through her when Paul told her so.

They made an elegant couple, she thought, as they entered the hotel foyer, where they were reflected in the mirrored walls. Paul wore a dark jacket and blue-checked slacks, with a blue silk polo-necked shirt. Together they looked like a young couple in love.

The thought embarrassed her all through dinner. So did the way their relationship seemed to be developing. Despite everything Paul had said and the official status she'd been given as P.R.O., Angela had the strongest suspicion that her real role was that of traveling companion. And several interpretations could be put on *that*.

Later she was introduced to Paris' clean and efficient Métro system. Because it followed the line of the streets, it was not as deep underground as some of London's systems. Paul asked her if there was any particular place she wanted to see.

"Montmartre," she said instantly. "The square where the artists paint, and the church of the Sacré Coeur."

He laughed softly. "I knew you were a romantic beneath all that efficiency. We'll have to walk the last part of the way then, as no buses or trains go up there. It's on a very steep hill, known as the *butte* of Montmartre."

"I suppose you're going to tell me you know the complete history of Montmartre as well," Angela challenged him as they boarded the Métro for the station nearest to the artists' quarter.

"All right, I know its history," he admitted with a grin. "This whole area was once covered with windmills, and Montmartre was a village of millers. At one time there was an endless procession of donkeys going up and down the cobbled streets, carrying corn up to the mills in the mornings and bringing down the milled flour in the evenings. Intriguing enough for a start?"

He could draw as vivid a picture as any artist, Angela thought grudgingly, knowing she wanted to hear more even though she was feeding his ego.

"Okay, then—why the name Montmartre?" she asked next.

"The Hill of Mercury, the Roman god, is the accepted explanation. Mercury was the god most revered by Parisians–lord of the arts–hence the connection with music and painting and all things Bohemian. *Voilà!*"

Angie laughed, her eyes sparkling. She was discovering what good company Paul could be when he wasn't giving her the old come on. But she might have known he couldn't resist commenting on her relaxed mood. He leaned toward her in the train, his brown eyes gleaming as brightly as hers.

"Right now I'd even exchange my career for that of an artist able to capture that particular look on your face forever," he said lightly, and then his voice deepened to the rich husky quality she always found so shiveringly disturbing, and his hand covered her own.

"There's nothing quite so beautiful, Angie, as the look of a lovely woman experiencing something for the first time—the way you're experiencing Paris."

His last words lessened the sudden tension she felt.

"I wish Tim could see it too." She brought his name up hurriedly and deliberately, and she saw a hard line replace the softness on Paul's sensual mouth. He didn't move away from her, but she sensed the distance between them in his brusque tone as she slid her hand away from his.

"I hardly think he's the type to appreciate the essence of Montmartre."

"You don't know him," Angela said, and then went on quickly, before he had the chance to start quizzing her about Tim's qualities. "Anyway, what do you call the essence of Montmartre? Tell me how it changed from a village high on a hill to become the center for artists it is today."

Paul shrugged. "All right. Imagine the windswept hill more than a century ago, a country village outside the city, difficult to reach because of its position. A few artists discovered it and its splendid views, and moved in. More followed, the way people always do. But these were serious artists, poor and struggling, and as Montmartre was cheap and quiet in those days, it became a kind of Mecca. And where artists go, poets and musicians follow. The living was casual and unhurried, and crazy goings-on took place to add to the growing Bohemian atmosphere of the place."

The train reached its destination, and Paul took her hand again to lead her out of the Métro station into the gathering dusk. Angela stayed close to his side as they walked steadily upward through the narrow streets of color-washed houses and street cafes, until the steep climb up the tiers of stone steps leading to the summit of the hill loomed ahead. She was glad of Paul's hand now. The faint sound of accordion music drifted down to them; there was a strong scent of flowery blossoms from the gardens nearby, and her anticipation was intense. She walked on silently to the top of the stone steps, and then the traces of annoyance in her mind vanished in an instant as she realized they were directly at one corner of the Place du Tertre, the square of the artists, and it was all spread out in front of them like a glowing tapestry of color.

"Oh!" she said softly. She stood quite still, wanting to savor the scene and imprint it on her memory. Maybe it would be brash and noisy in the daytime, but with the onset of evening the square took on a magical quality enhanced by the subtle lighting and muted music coming from the cafés, and the soft warmth of the summer night.

The whole square was softly illuminated. The center contained a café area, filled with checker-clothed tables and bright red umbrellas, at which sat couples interested only in each other. Around the perimeter of the square the artists were still at work, absorbed in their own world of oils and canvas and water colors. Canvases were stacked carelessly or propped reverently on easels.

"You would like a sketch of the pretty lady?"

A young male student stood in front of Angela, smiling appreciatively. A sketch block and charcoals were in his hands, and he gestured toward a cane chair in his own little corner of the square. Around the chair were a dozen charcoal sketches, all signed "Marcel." Other students carrying sketch blocks milled around the square plying for customers.

"I don't think so——" Angie began.

"How much?" Paul asked abruptly. Marcel quoted a sum that seemed exorbitant to Angela, but Paul was already nudging her toward the cane chair. Seated and positioned by the young student, she gazed over his shoulder to where Paul waited with an expressionless look on his face. She wanted to look away from him, but Marcel kept murmuring to her to remain still. He claimed that she was a perfect subject and the sketch would be *magnifique* because she was so lovely. Minutes later, he signed the sketch with a flourish and handed it to her.

As Angela glimpsed at it, her cheeks flushed. He'd made her beautiful, but there was more to it than that. She wore the look of a woman in love, and she hoped Paul wouldn't recognize it as such. After placing a piece of protective greaseproof paper over it, Marcel rolled the sketch up and secured the roll with an elastic band as Paul paid him.

"Mine, I think," she heard Paul say, taking it from Marcel's hand.

It was ridiculous to feel cheated, but Angie felt that somehow he'd captured a little part of her that should remain her secret. It was a feeling inspired by the aura of this place, Angie realized. The artists and the scented air, the muted accordion music drifting out of the cafes, all of these things were unobtrusive but seductive.

"I hope you'll give me my sketch," she spoke lightly as they moved away from Marcel's corner.

"I will not," Paul said calmly. "If you're so determined to keep up this pretence of an eternal passion for your insipid Tim, then at least I'll keep that one moment of your life all to myself."

She bit her lip, not daring to interpret his words. Her heart was thudding as he pulled her hand through his arm, steered her to a table and ordered them each a glass of wine. Montmartre was romance, and Paris was a place to be visited with someone very special . . . Angie was unwilling to admit that Paul could become someone *very* special to her, despite all her reservations.

She shivered, and Paul immediately said they'd better move on if she still wanted to see Sacré Coeur, which was just a short walk away. The night had deepened, and she was very glad Paul knew his way around so well. As they left the Place du Tertre, he still held her arm close to him. She couldn't think of anything to say as the accordion music receded. They weren't two ordinary tourists, and she was very conscious of it. There was no need for Paul to escort her about like this. She was only an employee. She stumbled slightly, and at once she was pressed closer to him as he stopped to steady her.

"Paul, I—I want to thank you for tonight——" she began confusedly.

His arms were around her at once. She knew he was going to kiss her and made no attempt to stop him. Why stop him, when it felt so right, so wonderful, to be held in his arms high above the city of Paris on a balmy night made for lovers?

"You don't need to thank me for anything," he murmured against her lips. "Not now or ever, sweet Angie."

The kiss didn't last more than a moment, and she was thankful he couldn't guess how much it stirred her.

Everything about him was so—so *exciting,* she thought, with a little catch in her breath. His personality, his touch, the magic of his music. . . . It was no wonder every woman fell a little in love with him. Why should she expect to be any exception?

They moved on toward the street where the church was situated, and everything else was forgotten as soon as Angie saw the glistening white domes rising skyward. The floodlit domes and facade of the church were so beautiful they brought a tight sensation to her throat. The exterior looked like a fairytale palace, and when they went inside it was like being in another world, cool and wide and tranquil. All around them the lovely stained glass windows held the dark mysteries of years gone by.

"I never dreamed it would be like this," Angela whispered. "I knew it was built of white stone, but it seems so—so pure."

"That's the idea," Paul said in a dry voice.

The worshippers were lighting candles. Some visitors knelt in silent prayer, others merely strolled around with curiosity. An old man stood motionless with a rosary in his hand. It was suddenly all too much for Angela to see such blatant emotion portrayed this way. She muttered that she had to get outside. The atmosphere was suddenly cloying.

Outside, the breeze that once turned the windmills of Montmartre still blew refreshingly, wafting the scent of blossoms to their nostrils. Angie drank it in deeply, and then she slowly looked around her to where the whole of Paris lay spread out below the *butte* of Montmartre like a giant canvas of twinkling lights. The total effect was of stunning beauty as the lights of Paris outlined the angles and contours of the city.

It was almost blasphemous to think of leaving here to return to the hotel and begin the tour. But she reminded herself that that was why she had come, and she sensed Paul was becoming impatient with acting the tourist, as he'd seen all this so many times before. She looked across the street to the place where they would begin the descent.

She was suddenly aware of a strange soft humming noise all around them. It had been hardly noticeable as they left the glorious facade of Sacré Coeur, but now, as they neared the steps, it grew louder. The steps were all shadowed from the blaze of light surrounding the white church. As Angela's eyes adjusted to the darkness, she discovered that they were covered with young people, softly strumming guitars and singing so quietly and dreamily that the sounds emerged as gently as a caress of the senses.

Emotion thickened in her throat as she listened. She felt Paul's arm around her waist, and his cheek close to hers. They couldn't break the spell of the music by treading a careful path through the musicians, and they stayed close together in the dimness of the steps without speaking until it ended.

"It's so beautiful." Her voice was ragged with emotion as the guitar notes faded away on the breeze. "It's indescribable. . . ."

"Thank you for letting me see it all again as if for the first time." His voice was suddenly as thick as hers, as he pulled her into his arms and pressed his mouth to hers with a passion that should have stunned her. Instead, she found herself winding her arms around him, and pressing her body to his. There was no other way she could have responded in this city made for lovers, in this most romantic spot of all, on the steps of Montmartre.

Chapter Four

Before she went down for breakfast the next morning, Angela studied the list Charlie Cass had given her before they left England. There was quite a lot of telephoning necessary to set up the press meetings and to enquire about the recording sessions, and she had to check with the Théatre des Fleurs about the availability of the hall for practice sessions for Paul.

"I'd better start on it right away," she told him over their continental breakfast of rolls and jam and coffee, "in case there are any problems. I presume I can use the phone in my room and have the calls charged to your account?"

"That's fine." He had been vague all morning, and Angela knew his mood was far removed from the one of the previous night when he'd kissed her so passionately. She breathed a small sigh of relief. It was best that it should be. The fact that his kisses had stirred her so much was neither here nor there. Their association was for business purposes. As if to play down her attractiveness and emphasize that fact, Angela had dressed soberly in a dark skirt and a high-necked cotton flowered blouse with cool beige sandals. She wore hardly any makeup, just a touch of lip gloss and eyeliner.

To her dismay, she needn't have bothered. Paul was a world away from her in spirit, and she assumed this was part of that strange temperament of his. Perhaps the music was already running through his head and all his attention was captured by it. Perhaps even a man with his strength of character and intensity had his attacks of nervous tension before a concert. Whatever the reason, Angela sensed it and respected it.

He told her he had some private calls to make that day, and probably wouldn't see her until late afternoon. He took a card from his wallet and handed it to her.

"Give Jacques a ring and see if it's still on for dinner with him tonight, will you, darling?"

He said the endearment so casually that it obviously meant nothing, though it gave her a little start to hear it on his lips. It was merely the easy endearment of a theater person, she reminded herself.

"Oh—and before you go, Paul, I understand I'll need a list of the pieces you intend to play at the Théatre des Fleurs for the program. I'd better see to that right away, hadn't I?"

"Sure." He handed her the key to his room. "You'll find it on the side table, together with some brief notes. I always like to give a few snippets about the composer if I can, but these aren't to be included in the program. It merely gives me something to say on the concert platform and saves me from just sitting there like a dummy while somebody else announces the pieces."

"You could never look like a dummy," Angela said involuntarily.

He smiled across the breakfast table and blew her an extravagant kiss.

"Thanks, darling. I love you too!" he said lightly. "I'm glad you remembered about the program. Get that phoned through first thing, will you? They can run them off quickly, but they start getting edgy if they don't get a couple of days' notice at least!"

She drank a third cup of coffee after he had left the hotel dining room. Her heart seemed to be leaping about in her chest. She had said the words often enough herself in that flippant way. "I love you too. ". . . ." It was another cliché which meant nothing in the mood in which it was spoken. And yet, for a moment there had been a wild surge of longing to hear them said sincerely, tenderly, from Paul's lips.

"The newspapers, Mademoiselle."

Angela gave a little start as a hotel clerk placed a small pile of newspapers at her side and she murmured her hurried thanks. They would be delivered daily, Charlie had told her, and she was supposed to skim through them for any mention of Paul, reviews or profiles or photographs, have them photocopied and sent back to London. It was also her job to see that there *were* such items, she reminded herself.

In her own room she skimmed through the list of piano pieces Paul intended to play. Predictably, they included the more popular classics, and some fairly modern tunes. The final piece was to be "Autumn Leaves." Angela stared at the words, wondering if this had been chosen deliberately on her account, and for what reason. She glanced curiously at what he called his "snippets." Her mouth twitched as she read his words about Franz Liszt in his strong hand, because they might have been describing Paul himself:

> his nature was full of conflict, which seems to have been reflected in his music, giving us moods of satanic brilliance and deep sensitivity . . . alternately tempestuous and charming . . .

The notes continued in the same vein, sometimes about the music itself, sometimes about the composer's background. Beside "Autumn Leaves" he had scrawled "this particular piece for a very special lady." Angela stared at the words. He couldn't mean *her,* and if he did, it was probably said in a moment of sarcasm. She put the papers down angrily and turned to the newspapers.

It wasn't hard to find news about Paul's arrival in the

music pages. Practically every newspaper had a photo of him with her beside him, and one had caught her looking adoringly into his eyes. In all reports she was his "charming companion" or his "new lovely lady companion" or even the "new girl in the handsome Paul Blake's life." The implications enraged her. Nowhere was she referred to as a business associate. The fact that they might not even have known didn't soothe her at all. They would be told as soon as she got on the phone to the press!

Her anger spurred her into action. She had already spent more time than she should browsing, and she picked up her notebook and the phone book and resolutely set to work. By lunchtime the interviews with reporters had been fixed; the recording company would be sending a car to collect Paul in the morning to discuss the LPs; she had found the name of a copying service with experience in handling the musical programs of the Théatre des Fleurs, and they'd assured her when she had dictated the list of piano pieces that they would have them ready within two days and sent to the theater; and she had arranged with the Théatre des Fleurs that the hall would be available for Paul each afternoon for two hours. Finally she rang Comte Jacques Vincennes at the number Paul had given her, and heard the pleasure in his voice when he realized who she was.

"Paul asked me to phone to see if your invitation for dinner this evening is still on." She smiled into the phone.

"But of course! In fact I have already taken the liberty of booking a table at a nightclub. I have also contacted someone I think you will be interested to meet, my dear Angela, and with whom I know Paul will be anxious to renew acquaintance; so there will be four of us."

"Am I allowed to ask who it is?"

He laughed. "I think I shall keep it as a surprise for

you both. Please tell Paul I will send a car for you at eight-thirty, and I look forward very much to seeing you again, Angela."

The phone clicked off before she could tell him that Paul would probably prefer to use the hired car. Angela glanced at her watch. The rest of the day was hers, except for taking the newspaper cuttings to the more modestly priced photocopying service where she could use the machine herself, and mail them off to Charlie. She would do that after lunch, she decided, and then she would find her way to the Théatre des Fleurs to see where Paul was to perform.

The hotel provided Angela with a tourist map showing points of interest. She had enjoyed a light salad lunch followed by the most delicious crêpes suzette she had ever tasted. It was a beautiful afternoon and she was able to complete her photocopying quickly.

She studied her map. The Théatre was on the other side of the river from the hotel, toward the Île de la Cité, the tiny island that held the Palais de Justice and the majestic splendor of Nôtre Dame.

Angela walked toward the entrance of the historic church, trying to remember that she was angry with Paul because of the impression he'd given the newshounds, whether willingly or not. Anyway, it was all for show, wasn't it? She was just an employee, and useful to have around when the female audience became overly attentive. But the *ego* of it!

Maybe it was her change of mood, but the interior of Nôtre Dame didn't impress her the way Sacré Coeur had impressed her. It was bleak and gloomy, with little groups chanting away or with heads bent in silent prayer, and though other tourists were obviously awed by its grandeur, Angela was glad to be out in the sunlight again, to feel its warmth on her bare arms.

She was surprised to see how the time had raced away. She took the nearest Métro to the avenue des

Fleurs, a long, tree-lined road with the ornate façade of the Théatre at the end, its delicate filigree work and entwined cherubs over the entrance picked out in gilt. It was a magnificent façade, and Angela felt a little thrill of pleasure that she was to play a small part in Paul's appearance there.

She made herself known with an explanation about the programs, and was ushered around as if she were royalty, to her amusement. The manager was a round, dark little man who almost bowed away from her. He showed her his domain personally, an anxious look in his eyes as she inspected the plush dressing room and backstage where the small reception party would be held on Paul's last night. Finally M. Marcel allowed her onto the stage, where a beautiful ebony grand piano took pride of place.

Angela almost reeled. She had never stood on an empty stage before. Gazing out at what seemed thousands of empty seats, rising away from her in dozens of tiers, the curving balcony seemed so close she could almost reach up and touch it. For the first time she appreciated how Paul must feel, alone on that stage, with those seats filled with expectant people. No wonder the adrenaline flowed and his temperament erupted. Her admiration of him doubled for the sheer nerve of it all. It wasn't enough merely to have talent. It took guts to perform as a solo artist for a couple of hours, and then to be at the mercy of the critics the next day. She felt herself mellowing toward him.

When she returned to the hotel, all her fine feelings vanished as she saw him stride toward her in the foyer, a scowl on his handsome face.

"Where the devil have you been?" he said aggressively. "I suppose you didn't have enough sense to hand in my room key at the desk!"

Angela felt her face flush.

"They must have a master key——"

"Of course they do, but that's not the point, is it? I

expect a little efficiency now and then. And I also expect you to be here to tell me what you've accomplished today, if anything. I presume you haven't been gallivanting round sight-seeing *all* day?"

His eyes were on her bare arms, turning a golden color from her walks in the sun. Angela controlled her temper with an effort.

"Paris is quite a large city when you haven't been here before," she said shortly. "I've done everything you asked me to do, including confirming the dinner for this evening with your friend the count. He's sending a car, and there will be four of us. He wouldn't say who the other person would be. Can we sit down while I tell you of the week's arrangements, or are we going to stand here glaring at each other for all the hotel staff to see?"

Rudeness seemed to be the only way to handle this impossible man when he was at his most arrogant, Angela decided. It seemed to be the only thing he understood.

"I apologize," he said stiffly. He caught her arm and led her to a large sofa at one corner of the foyer. "Tell me what success you've had today."

He had evidently ordered afternoon tea to be served to them as soon as Angela appeared, for before she could begin a waitress came to tell them it was in Paul's suite. Angela looked at him suspiciously.

"I thought it would be more pleasant to take tea on my balcony rather than in the hotel dining room." His voice dismissed the idea of any ulterior motive in the suggestion.

Could this really be the man who could be so gentle and so sensitive? she found herself wondering almost savagely. The man who could project such warmth to an audience that they were his willing captives? She remembered the time at his house and moved a fraction farther away from him. But she needn't have worried. Thoughts of seduction were clearly nowhere in his mind. She handed him his room key without a word and followed him into his suite. A pot of tea and a selection of the most appetizing cakes and pastries were waiting for them on a small table on Paul's balcony.

He suddenly put both hands on her bare arms.

"Forgive me, Angela. I know I can be a real swine for the few days before a big concert. I keep forgetting that you aren't used to it the way Margaret was. She knew very well it would all blow over as soon as the first performance had come and gone. We seem to have known each other such a long time, somehow. I forget you're still new to the game."

At the unexpected gentleness in his voice her resentment fizzled out. He was looking at her with a lost-little-boy look in his brown eyes, a pleading look of someone who wanted most of all to be loved. A startling reaction was spinning through Angela's senses as his hands tightened on her arms. Not the reaction of an admirer looking adoringly from afar at her idol . . .

Something far more basic was stirring inside her. She felt a wild urge to fling her arms round his neck and tell him it didn't matter if he got angry and yelled at her, just as long as he softened toward her afterward, the way he was doing now; just as long as his mouth became tender and all his virile appeal was directed solely at her so that she could imagine just for a little while that he really felt something for her. Almost before the thoughts were clearly formulated in her mind his arms had slid around her, pulling her toward him. His mouth was on hers and her own arms were reaching around his neck, wanting him closer.

"You're a very desirable woman, Angela," he was murmuring against her lips. "I'm not sure which Angela I find the most exciting, the one with sparks flying in her eyes or the one who's vulnerable and childlike and looks about ready to burst into tears when I get stroppy!"

She laughed shakily. "I assure you I'm not a child, and I never cry." *Well, almost never,* she thought.

"No, you're not a child. You're all woman, and a very delicious one. I'd hate to be traveling around with a dragon, even though you can spit fire with the best of them sometimes."

He was suddenly teasing. It jarred on her a little, just when she was feeling her most relaxed with him, ready to play whatever game he chose—only not this one. She was remembering Charlie Cass's remark that she'd keep off the stage-door followers, and wondered if this was the little game Paul was about to pursue. The concert wasn't far off, and the press interviews were still to come. What could be better for his image than to have an adoring assistant hanging on his every word, obviously looking as if she were more than a mere assistant?

A little shiver ran through her. Paul's whole attitude at that moment was one of subtle triumph. His arms still held her captive, his fingers roamed seductively up and down her tense back, his body warm against her own. She felt every contour of it through the thin summer clothes she wore, and his own lightweight clothes. She pushed away from him. She had no wish to be some sort of decoy girlfriend, and no intention of letting him practice on her in private, if that was his intention.

"I don't think my boyfriend would approve of your strong-arm tactics." She strove to sound amused, as if his touch hadn't sent a wave of answering desire through her that shook her. She walked out to the balcony and picked up the teapot without turning to look at Paul, knowing his face would be darkening with anger again. He liked to be the one to do the teasing, she realized.

His arms suddenly caught hold of her around the waist again as he stood close behind her.

"I shall drop this teapot in a minute," she said angrily.

"Then put the blasted thing down! Do you think I'm going to play second fiddle to a teapot! Or to any half-witted boyfriend who hasn't got the gumption to keep you by his side?"

Angela kept her hold on the teapot, despite the fact that his lips were nuzzling into her neck, and the tingling was beginning again as the warmth of his skin touched hers. She hoped he wouldn't guess how fast her heart was beating, but she couldn't hide it from him when his hands slid easily beneath the thin cotton top she wore—though it wasn't her heart his fingers were seeking.

For a few heady seconds she allowed her head to lean back against his chest, aware that Paul's own heart was thudding more loudly than usual. Maybe this was all part of the treatment needed to keep the adrenaline flowing. His hands cupped her breasts as if they were made of yielding velvet.

"You're so beautiful, Angela," his voice whispered in her ear. "Every lovely inch of you, what I've seen so far!"

His words jolted her back to reality. She dumped the teapot on the small table and wrenched away from his caressing hands.

"Is this how you kept your Margaret with you for so long?" she said harshly. "Was she content to play the rôle of mistress as well as your assistant? I assure you not every woman is ready to fall for it, Mr. Blake."

She slopped milk into the cups with unsteady hands and topped them with tea. Paul didn't answer and she could almost feel the antagonism between them again. He turned on his heel to go back into his room and moments later he handed her a small file.

"Take a look," he snapped. "You'll find enough cuttings in there to convince you, I hope. Unless you imagine I'm the type of man who would seduce his own mother!"

Angela opened the file with misgivings as Paul sank his teeth into a crumbly French pastry, his eyes watching her. There were typical newspaper reports of his arrivals at concerts or airports, similar to the ones she'd seen that morning, but accompanying him was a round cheerful little woman with iron-gray hair. To dispel the last doubt, there was a wedding photograph of the same woman and a broadly smiling man of about the same age in an American newspaper cutting. Underneath was the caption "The nuptials of Texas oilman Harve Kellerman to Miss Margaret Lane of England."

Angela felt completely floored, and slightly ridiculous for reacting like a frightened rabbit the way she had. Truth to tell, she had never expected to feel so violently attracted to Paul Blake, and the force of her own reactions unnerved her. He was so obviously a ladies' man, loving all and true to none, and that type had always scared her off. There was no future with a man like that, not a lasting, fulfilling future.

"I'm sorry," she handed back the file, her voice small and embarrassed. "I had no idea, of course——"

"No, you did not, so you chose to think the worst of me. I wonder why that is." He looked at her coolly, as if she were under inspection. Angela flushed.

"Perhaps because I don't think much of a man who plays up to a girl he knows very well is attached to someone else," she whipped back. She reached for an eclair, more calmly than she felt. She no longer worried that she would anger him by answering back. He seemed to thrive on it.

"In that case, I'd better leave you strictly alone, except in the cause of business, hadn't I? Though it's a pity: we could have made such beautiful music together, and I'm not talking about the sort I play on the piano! But so be it. Tell me about your day."

Paul's mood switched abruptly, his face remote. Angela breathed a small sigh of relief, relating all that she had done on his behalf that day. And yet, incongruously, she longed to see that sudden smile light up his face, and the gentleness return to his eyes. He approved all her arrangements and finished his tea, stood up as if he couldn't get rid of her quickly enough, and told her he'd see her in the foyer in time for their dinner that evening.

Angela felt as deflated as a spent balloon when she went back to her own room, her nerves frayed at the edges. She reminded herself that he was brittle tempered because of the concert, and that once it was over he'd relax. Also, once she was used to his way of things, she'd understand and be able to cope.

She wilted on her bed. She'd *never* be able to cope. Working for a big company had been very different. Then, of course, she hadn't been so closely involved with her boss. Oh, there had been passes made at her. It was a natural hazard of the job, and she'd have started doubting her own femininity if it *hadn't* happened occasionally, but it had never made such an assault on her emotions as Paul Blake made. It had never mattered as much before. She had never cared so much.

She caught sight of her own white face in the dressing-table mirror, and her body, still taut and tense from the last half hour with Paul. She felt a swift urge to feel his arms around her again, holding her in his embrace, feeling the hardness of his body pressing against hers with an urgency that sent a wild sweet thrill coursing through her. It was no more than an automatic reaction to the aggressive maleness of such a man, she told herself desperately.

But she knew it was much, much more than that. No matter how hard she tried to resist it, she knew she was falling in love with Paul. That was the last thing on earth she wanted to do, to risk ending up as one of his castoffs. To Angela, love was a deep and lasting commitment, not just a momentary pleasure as it would seem to Paul. If she let it develop any further, she was headed for heartbreak, and she knew it. But knowing now her vulnerability where he was concerned, she would be doubly careful.

If he started a relentless loving campaign, she must laugh it all back in his face to subdue that great ego of his. It would be the only way she could continue to work for him.

Chapter Five

Her sixth sense should have warned her that the fourth member of the dinner party that evening would be Claudette Dubois.

Paul made no comment on Angela's appearance that evening, even though she knew she looked good enough to attract admiring glances from other men in the foyer of the hotel as they waited together for Jacques Vincennes' chauffeur. Her chin jutted out defiantly. She could have noted that Paul also looked his devastating best, in formal evening clothes with a frilled white shirt and velvet bow tie. But she would not let her thoughts even register the fact, and they sat stiffly side by side in the back of the sleek limousine. Side by side, and yet worlds apart.

It was ridiculous, Angela told herself angrily. They had known each other such a little time, but Paul was the kind of man who attracted instant reaction, whether good or bad. So far, most of his effect on her had been bad. She wouldn't let herself remember the sensual, almost erotic effect his music had on her when it seemed he played especially for her.

The limousine deposited them at an exclusive little nightclub where there was a floor show, and Jacques and the woman Angela recognized instantly from the photograph in Paul's London home stood waiting for them. Claudette looked breathtakingly gorgeous. Stark white silk caressed that voluptuous figure, clasped at the waist by a magnificent diamond clip. More diamonds dazzled at her throat, and her sleek black hair was caught up in a sophisticated knot on her head. Her dark eyes swept over Angela and dismissed her while the smile never left her lips as she walked toward Paul with outstretched arms and embraced him rapturously.

"*Chéri*, it has been too long!" she announced in her rich voice. Though she did not speak English as perfectly as Jacques, on her the accent was unbelievably sexy. Predictably Paul responded at once. Suddenly, as if someone had switched him on, his face became alive as he and the opera singer greeted each other with more affection than seemed necessary for mere friends. It might have been no more than the way theatrical people behaved, Angela thought, but searing jealousy ran through her like a flame as she watched them together.

Seconds later she too was caught up in Jacques Vincennes' brand of continental charm. He was not quite as effusive as the other two, but her hand was being kissed by the charming Frenchman, who was giving her all the compliments she could wish for.

"You look very lovely tonight, Angela," Jacques told her, his eyes lingering approvingly in all the appropriate places. "That soft rose color suits you to perfection. The décolleté is going to distract me from eating, but the feast for my eyes will be sweeter than the cuisine."

His flattery was outrageous and flamboyant, but she couldn't take it seriously. And the rose-pink evening gown with its little straps tied on the shoulders and deep neckline had seemed so elegant until she came face to face with the ice-cold beauty of Claudette Dubois. Now she felt suddenly gauche and young.

Jacques made the introductions between the two of them and then led the way to their table in the center of the floor. There was no hiding away for two famous stars, Angela realized. And indeed, halfway through the evening, the spotlight normally reserved for the floor show rested on their table, with the announcement that the establishment was honored by the presence of two distinguished guests that evening: their own adored Claudette Dubois, who was about to perform in *La Bohème* in Copenhagen, and the English pianist, Paul Blake, whose concerts in Paris would be at the Théatre des Fleurs.

The two of them stood holding hands while they received the applause. It was like watching a bridal couple, Angela thought sickly, with Claudette in that white gown and Paul so dark and handsome. He leaned across and kissed her cheek before they sat down at the table again and the spotlight roamed on to spot lesser celebrities.

The jealousy burned on inside Angie, futile though it was. The one bright spot was the reference to Claudette going to Copenhagen. Her effusiveness was overpowering, and Angela knew she wouldn't want to be around the singer for very long—especially when Paul appeared so besotted by her. It surprised Angela. She hadn't expected him to be so gushing. She was slightly disappointed in him, until she happened to catch him glancing her way with a sardonic expression on his face. Then she knew. He was doing this deliberately, because of the way she'd rejected him earlier. The realization hit her with a little shock.

Why should it matter to him anyway? She was just one woman, and his employee at that. Why should one minor conquest that he lost make him worry when he could have the world at his feet if he wanted it?

She certainly wasn't going to let him see it ruffled her that he gave all his attention to Claudette. She didn't need to, when Jacques was clearly more than happy to act as her special companion, even though Angela hadn't quite expected them to divide into couples in this way. But Paul danced with Claudette when the meal was over, and Angela gave all *her* attention to the elegant Jacques.

"Dance with me," Jacques said quietly. "A lovely lady shouldn't have that sad look in her eyes on a night out in Paris. This is the city for lovers, or at the very least, for pretending to be in love. Don't you remember the words of the song, Angela? If you can't be with the one you love, then love the one you're with!"

He was teasing her, not realizing how her heart jolted at his words. She'd started out with the one she loved, she thought tremulously, but now she had to watch him dance with another woman, who was obviously enjoying the experience. And from the way they acted together, it was obvious too that they were very familiar with each other. The thought depressed her. They made a striking couple. Claudette was nearly as tall as Paul, her cheek touching his as they moved slowly in time to the music. Angela tried to ignore the bleakness inside her as Jacques held her close.

Later, Paul abruptly interrupted, saying that it was time they changed partners or Jacques would begin to think he was monopolizing Claudette all evening. It wasn't exactly a gracious request to dance, and Angela's instincts were to refuse. Still, she couldn't deny herself a legitimate chance to be held in his arms without the onslaught on her emotions, as he could hardly try to seduce her on the dance floor.

She needn't have worried. Held in his arms, she was still as far away as he'd been in the limousine. He hadn't forgiven her for rejecting him. But if he intended to punish her by his coldness, he had not reckoned on the close proximity of the crowded dance floor, and the fact that Angela felt so deliciously warm and pliant in his arms. She wasn't as tall as Claudette, and the soft cloud of her gold-brown hair tickled his cheek. She wore a tantalizing perfume that rose in his nostrils and stirred his senses. He could feel her round taut curves against him and his hand tightened against the hollow of her back. His lips brushed her cheek and stayed there, sensual against her skin.

"Why do you resist me when I want you so much?" he murmured.

Angela swayed against him, feeling the rapid beat of his heart against her own. Didn't he sense that she wanted him too? That she was every bit as aroused by him as he was by her? But wanting wasn't loving, and she needed to be loved.

"You *will* give in," he said softly, when she stayed silent, a catch in her throat because she knew she could give this man so much love if only the love was mutual. "I promise you I'll make you mine before this tour's ended."

Angela looked up slowly into the arrogant eyes that looked down so imperiously into her own. She was imagining for a moment how it would feel to know the abandonment of his caresses and the rapture of possessing and being possessed . . . but for how long? As long as it suited him to toy with his assistant, presumably. Someone to be there on his tours, when some other sophisticated beauty such as Claudette Dubois wasn't around to fan his desires. Perhaps even now it was Claudette who really held his heart, but Angela was like a thorn in his flesh that he had to remove by proving that she would give in to him eventually.

She opened her mouth to taunt him with some scathing remark, when his mouth suddenly descended on hers. The lights were so dim and the dance floor so crowded it would be hardly noticed, and if it was, Paris was the city for lovers, and surely no one would mind! It was more than Angela could do to pretend indifference. She suddenly longed for Paul's touch with a passion that shook her, and she was hardly aware how eagerly she returned his kiss.

"Can you really tell me that meant nothing to you?"

Paul murmured as he moved his lips a fraction from hers. "If you do, I'll have to call you a liar, my sweet Angela. Deny if you can that you suddenly came alive a few seconds ago. And then tell me if your precious Tim ever made you feel like that!"

She didn't answer. She leaned her head weakly against his shoulder, knowing only too well that no one had ever made her feel the way Paul Blake did. Certainly not Tim.

If she had ever believed she was in love with Tim, this brief time with Paul had taught her that her earlier feelings were like a mild summer breeze compared to a hurricane. She had been unaware that she was even capable of such feelings until now.

But Paul would never know, she vowed feverishly. She couldn't bear to have the pretence of his love, and then have it all turn to ashes when he tired of her. From now on she must try to keep an even tighter rein on her emotions whenever he pursued her this way.

"I told you," she said as steadily as she could. "Tim has been part of my life for a long time. What I feel for him is untouchable."

It was the truth, but she hoped her choice of words would mislead him. She wanted Paul to assume that she and Tim had an understanding and a future together that could discount any outside temptation. She hoped she managed to sound a little contemptuous, as if she knew very well what Paul was trying to do, and she knew just how to deal with his type. She had the satisfaction of seeing the anger flare in his eyes as the lights resumed their subtle glow and the dance music ended in time for the cabaret. He led her back to their table, his grip on her elbow cruelly firm.

"And what I feel for you is undeniable," he spoke in a harsh whisper in her ear. "I'm not used to being refused."

His tone said he wouldn't give up either, she thought

weakly. She sat down abruptly and sipped at her glass of wine, feeling her cheeks burn as Claudette looked at her thoughtfully, as if she knew exactly what had been happening between her and Paul. It was a look that was slightly incredulous too, that wondered how such a charismatic man could be attracted to this pretty little English girl when the Junoesque Claudette was around. The opera singer's eyes moved to Paul now, the dazzling smile back on her face, her full red lips parted in a gleaming smile of welcome.

"Jacques and I have something to suggest," she announced. Angela's heart lurched. Somehow she knew she wasn't going to like the suggestion. "As you know, *chéri*, I'm off to Copenhagen tomorrow for ten days, and then I will come back to Paris for a television appearance and an interview for Jacques's magazine. He has been wanting to do a profile on me for some time now, so that will all take another couple of weeks, I expect, because I have to see my designer about some new clothes for the autumn season."

How the rich lived, Angela thought, though she couldn't quite see what this had to do with Paul. She was only glad that Claudette's assignments in Paris didn't coincide with their own. The singer annoyed her.

"What *ma belle* Claudette is getting round to slowly," Jacques put in with an affectionate laugh, "is that when you have finished your tour, Paul, I gather you will be in Marseille, is that right?"

Paul nodded. "And in need of a holiday! In fact, the last week is free. We shall either relax in Marseille, or give press interviews if required, or go straight back to England if we both feel we've had enough by then."

Angela didn't look at him. She hadn't realized the last week was as flexible as that. Charlie Cass had mentioned vaguely that the press would be looking to her for interviews, and the hope of getting Paul on a TV chat show, and she had assumed that would be the end of it. A week's holiday hadn't been on her itinerary. She acknowledged that Paul would need one by then, and she might too—but not in his exclusive company. Not when she felt so defenseless in his presence.

"Then I want you both to join me at a small house party," Jacques went on. "Claudette has already said she will be able to make it, and I would be charmed to show Angela round my home. Have you ever visited the Camargue, *chérie?*"

Her interest was caught, despite the dismay she felt at the proposed reunion of the four of them. But hopefully, a house party given by Comte Vincennes would be a larger affair than a cozy foursome.

"No I haven't, though I've heard of it. Isn't that where the wild white horses roam? And bull fights——" she sought in her memory for all she'd ever heard of the mysterious, haunting area of France, bleak and unforgiving compared to the lushness of its near neighbors, the southern resorts of the Riviera, yet luring with a fascination that drew the tourists with avid curiosity. She heard Claudette give an amused laugh.

"Our little Angela is a romantic!" she said. From her the words sounded as if she were bestowing a gracious favor on a child. Angela felt her face redden and was angry at the knowledge.

"I'm merely repeating the few things I've been told about the area," she said coolly. She was aware that the two men were watching the little exchange and noticing the clash of personalities for the first time. She turned away from Claudette's brittle beauty and spoke to Jacques. "Am I so wrong?" she challenged.

He squeezed her small hand as it lay on the table and raised it gallantly to his lips. His eyes met hers above the caress.

"You are not, *chérie*. And neither should you be ashamed of being a romantic. It always shows in the face of such a woman and heightens her femininity.

Men will always be attracted to a gentle woman. So, it is settled then, if Paul has no objections. The last week of your tour, providing you are free, you will come to the Château Vincennes near Arles. I will arrange for half a dozen other guests to join us so it will be an interesting gathering."

Angela had hardly dared glance at Claudette while Jacques was talking. No one could call *her* a gentle woman, for all her blatant beauty, and she hoped the singer hadn't felt Jacques was making a dig at her. But apparently not. Claudette's laugh trilled out again as she hugged Paul's arm possessively.

"You won't need to ask Paul twice, Jacques! It will be the climax to a most successful French tour. And don't tell me I am tempting fate to call it successful when it has not even begun yet. You cannot fail, my darling, and you know it!"

She blew an extravagant kiss in Paul's direction, and he replied dryly that since it all seemed to be cut and dried he'd better not be the one to voice any objection. He added to Jacques that of course he was delighted by the invitation and accepted on behalf of himself and Angela.

If the last week were to be free, she might have felt inclined to go straight back to England, she found herself thinking. At any rate it would have been nice to have the choice. She had the surest feeling that by the time the tour ended she'd have had as much as she could take, if Paul continued his seduction campaign. In her heart she had already been half forming her letter of formal resignation, knowing this tour would have to be her one and only commitment with Paul Blake.

He was watching her face, and she knew he could read her mind at that moment. She hoped desperately he couldn't read the whole truth, that she was already so much in love with him she couldn't bear to be around when he turned his roving eye on someone else. Thankfully the lights dimmed at that moment and the evening's cabaret began.

Angela was able to study his handsome profile as it was silhouetted in shadow. It was a strong face, with a firm angular chin and a well-shaped head. She knew its contours by heart, and yet she wanted to keep looking at it. As if he was aware of it, he turned and looked her way, his mouth relaxing into a small smile as he did so. She wondered if he was remembering that sensuous kiss on the dance floor.

By the time the limousine took them back to their hotel, Angela was so sleepy she had difficulty in keeping her head from lolling against Paul's shoulder. But resist she did. They stumbled into the hotel foyer, where only the night porter smiled vacantly at them, and took the lift to their rooms.

"A nightcap before bed, I think," Paul said as they stood in the corridor.

"You won't get room service at this hour," she told him. In any case, she had no wish for any more wine. What she'd had already was spinning round in her head. She tried to pass him on the way to her own room, but as they reached his door, his hand grasped her arm tightly.

"There's champagne and glasses in my room, and it's been chilling in the fridge all evening. Come and help me drink it," he said softly.

It was all ready and waiting. He'd been so sure of her, she raged. So sure she'd be unable to go on saying no. His fingers moved slowly up and down her arm. She felt the skin tingle where he touched it.

"Are you afraid?" His voice seemed to reach her from a distance.

Angela shook herself mentally. No, she was not afraid. She could either stalk off to bed like a frightened virgin, or prove to Paul that she was perfectly capable of drinking a glass of champagne with him and then bidding him a cool goodnight, no matter how differently he visualized the ending to this evening.

"Lead the way," she replied steadily.

He looked a little surprised at her sudden capitulation, and unlocked his door quickly before she could change her mind. She dropped her silky shawl and evening bag on the bed and moved away to sit on one of the velvet-covered bedroom chairs. Paul didn't miss the way she behaved, calm on the outside but with small jerky movements that betrayed her nervousness.

She intrigued him more than any woman he'd ever known, his Angela with the tip-tilted nose that was so endearing. She had the artlessness of a child at times, and yet the warmth of a very sensual woman who hadn't yet been fully unleashed. Paul badly wanted to be the one to discover just how pleasurable it would be to arouse her to her own sensuality. The thought was both stimulating and exciting to him. He had known many women, but never one who could rouse him to anger or tenderness with such apparent ingenuousness.

He opened the little fridge and withdrew a bottle of champagne in its ice bucket and two glasses. He wiped the glasses carefully on a cloth before filling them with champagne and handing one to Angela.

"To us," he said softly. "To business and something more than friendship."

He held out his glass to hers, and after a moment she touched her own glass to his before she took a drink. There was an air of *fait accompli* in his words, she thought, but she was still in control of herself and intended to stay in control. The champagne was ice-cold and slid down her throat deliciously. The bubbles burst against her nose, and the sensation was as heady as the wine.

Paul was pushing a cassette into the portable recorder he had with him, and the next minute the strains of his own performance of "Autumn Leaves" was filling the room, softly and seductively.

"Oh, that's not fair," she whispered.

He didn't answer. He turned out all the lights but one bedside lamp that glowed with a warm soft glow over the luxurious room. He put down his glass and held out his hand to her.

"Come and dance with me again," he said slowly.

She did as she was told. Her slender high heels caught in the thick carpet, and after a few seconds she kicked them off. She was warmed by his arms and the feeling of well-being that was spreading languorously through her now. Her arms were around his neck, their bodies so close she could feel the hard strength of his chest, his taut stomach muscles, the corded masculinity of him against her thighs.

"Why have you held out against me for so long, Angela?" Paul murmured, his lips warm against her cheek.

She swallowed. "Because—I—I must——"

He touched her mouth with those little ghost kisses that stirred her senses so exquisitely. She half expected him to become aggressively demanding at her hesitance, but he didn't.

"Why must you? Not because of some foolish sense of loyalty to Tim? I won't believe he was ever that important to you when everything about you is telling me differently." Usually the sound of Tim's name could make him angry, yet he had used it himself, as if it was meaningless to him. His voice was strangely gentle, as caring as the perfect tender lover. He was dangerously seductive.

"Paul, this mustn't happen——" Her voice was weakening, and she knew how desperately hard it would be to refuse him anything he wanted.

His kiss stopped her speaking again, with little

pressure from his lips. Just enough to keep her wanting more, as the rippling sounds of his music filled her head and his charisma enveloped her totally.

"Must is a word I'd take out of the vocabulary," Paul said softly. "Unless it's to say that it's time you stopped listening to your head, and you must listen to your heart instead."

"Is that what you're doing?" Angela said unsteadily. It was becoming difficult to think straight, with his hands gently caressing her in this semblance of a dance.

"Of course." His voice was a seductive whisper against her cheek. "And my heart tells me you're the loveliest, most desirable woman ever to come into my life. From the first moment I saw you, no one else existed for me, my darling."

The blood flowed more quickly in her veins as he called her his darling. It was what she wanted to be . . . to be his, to belong to him utterly, now and for always. Paul's arms were holding her very close, keeping her safe, as she drifted on a warm blue silken sea.

"Are you really so uncaring as you pretend, my lovely Angela?" he said huskily, as they moved very slowly to the music.

"Oh, no—no," she breathed out the words in a long sigh. She wasn't uncaring at all, and never could be as far as Paul was concerned. She lifted a trembling hand to the heat in her cheeks, knowing she was becoming completely bemused by the nearness of him, and these surroundings, so intimately Paul's. The room was a warm haze, but everywhere she looked it spoke of him.

When he kissed her, she no longer attempted to resist, only pulled him closer to her. When his hands reached out for the silky ties on the rose pink gown and his lips moved to touch the softness of her breasts, she almost held her breath.

She was in a dream world, incapable of thought. She was where she most wanted to be, in the arms of the man she loved.

"My bed is big enough for two, darling," he murmured against her throat. "I want to see your hair spread out on my pillow and wake up with you still in my arms. I want you so much, my sweet Angela."

He was propelling her gently toward the bed, each word punctuated by a gentle kiss that made her tingle down to her toes. Why not? she could hear the insistent urging inside her head. Why not, when they both wanted it so much.

The cassette came abruptly to an end, with only the soft rustling of the tape whirring round on the spool. Angela could feel the rounded edge of the bed behind her knees as Paul gave a smothered oath and left her momentarily to stride across the room to turn the tape over to play the other side.

In those few moments all Angela's resolve returned to her. He had engineered all this for the sole purpose of seducing her. There had been no mention of love. He wanted her and that was all. His ego couldn't believe that she wouldn't submit. Within seconds she had gathered up her shawl and her evening bag and scooped up her shoes. Before he realized what she was doing she had sped to the door, opened it, and escaped into the corridor. She ran to her own room, turned the key with shaking hands and leaned against the door, her heart thumping so wildly she thought she was going to pass out for a moment.

She heard him tap angrily on the other side of the door.

"Angela, come out of there." His voice was furious, though suitably subdued. He wouldn't want to rouse the whole hotel and cause a scandal. He had his reputation to think about. She counted on that as she stood there, unmoving, for the few minutes he pleaded. Finally, there was no more sound. He wouldn't beg forever. He wasn't that kind of man.

Eventually she moved away from the door and undressed with trembling hands. If the cassette hadn't stopped, she knew very well she'd have spent the night in Paul's arms. The realization made her alternately enraged at his trickery to get her there, and at the undoubted emptiness and frustration, when fulfillment had so nearly been hers for the taking.

What kind of fool was she? she asked herself. Any other girl would have leaped at the chance if Paul had charmed her the way he'd charmed Angela. He was everything she ever wanted, and she had thrown it all away because of that little word called love. If only he had said he loved her. Whether he'd meant it or not, she'd have believed it for the moment, and she wouldn't be crawling into a cold and lonely bed, aching with a longing such as she'd never known before.

She never cried, Angela reminded herself fiercely, and she wouldn't cry now. But long after she'd drifted into a fretful sleep her cheeks were flushed and her pillow was damp.

Chapter Six

The next morning Angela awoke with a throbbing headache. She was anxious about seeing Paul at breakfast, but relied on the fact that there was too much for them to do that day for him to be able to brood over her running out on him last night. And there was something she'd forgotten to arrange: Charlie had given her the name of a photographer who would run off a batch of give-away photos for Paul to sign on request after the concerts at the Théatre des Fleurs. She broached the subject as soon as she saw him, glad to have a topic to discuss.

He nodded coldly. "You'd better get on to it right away. I can't disappoint my fans. Maybe you'd like one too, since you can't accept the real thing."

He was like a petulant, small boy, Angela thought angrily.

"If we're going to argue the whole time, perhaps it would be better if you found another assistant," she began.

"I don't want another assistant. I've told you enough times—I want you." His words were blunt, heavy with double meaning. "And don't think you can get out of our contract so easily. You agreed to do this complete tour with me. I can't start looking for somebody else in the middle of it! And the whole tour includes the week at the end at Jacques's place, so don't think you're going to skip off and leave me again. You'll enjoy that anyway. Plenty of people around to safeguard your honor, and the luxury of the château to relax in.''

He couldn't resist the sarcasm. Angela looked pointedly at her watch.

"You're supposed to be at the recording studio at ten-thirty," she reminded him. "I don't know how far away it is——"

"I'd better go." He drained his coffee. "You've got the address of the photographer and the photo Charlie and I selected for this tour, haven't you? When you've seen to it, take a taxi and join me later. They'll no doubt lay on lunch for us and maybe give us a look round if you're interested."

She was. They parted company, Angela with a feeling of relief that business had taken over the antagonism between them resulting from last night's clash. Paul had hardly left the hotel when she was paged. Jacques was waiting for her in the foyer.

"I should have mentioned that I'd like to be around for today's recording session," he greeted her. "For the profile for my magazine, you understand. Readers love to see the artists actually at work, behind the scenes, so to speak. I'm no mean photographer myself."

He waggled a camera about disarmingly. For a count, he was extraordinarily natural, Angela thought, feeling herself warm toward him. He was the same type as Tim, she realized suddenly, which probably accounted for her finding him so appealing. It wasn't anything sexual, but a brotherly affection—which was not the way Tim had wanted her to feel, she thought ruefully.

"I'm not sure what's happening at the recording studios, Jacques," she told him. She also mentioned briefly what she was about to do and he immediately offered to chauffeur her around himself.

"If we're both going to end up at the studios, it makes sense, doesn't it? And I'm not going to deprive myself of the chance of having you to myself for a while, *chérie!* When Paul's around, most lovely ladies have eyes for no one but him."

"I'm sure that's not true," Angela protested, because Jacques was a highly personable young man, apart from his obvious wealth and position. But he laughed good-naturedly.

"In some cases, yes!" he admitted. "But in your case, I think Paul has already won your heart, no? A reporter is trained to be observant in all things, and a Frenchman is especially observant in affairs of the heart."

He spoke teasingly again, but Angela had the feeling he knew very well the way her feelings were being torn apart because of Paul. Perhaps he'd seen it all before. If he knew Paul well, he'd be well aware of the way he operated. She could hardly pump Jacques for information, but maybe if she hinted, she could glean a bit more about the real Paul Blake.

"I'd be happy to take you up on your offer," she said quickly. "I'll just fetch my jacket."

Jacques didn't miss the glibness in her voice and he watched her thoughtfully as she went toward the lift. Her delightful shape, he thought, and that glorious hair reminded him of ripening corn. Everything about Miss Angela Raines was soft and curvy and highly desirable, and he envied his old friend, even if he was such a dunderhead as to be unaware that his new assistant was head over heels in love with him. Englishmen were oddly slow in realizing such things, Jacques Vincennes thought indulgently.

Angela reappeared with her portfolio. There were complimentary tickets to send out to the press and the small list of notables Charlie had given her. It wouldn't do to forget those. She saw them safely into the hotel mailbox and smiled at Jacques.

"Right. Now I'm all yours."

"Oh, you English," he grinned. "You say these

emotive phrases without thinking how a Frenchman takes their meaning literally."

Angela laughed at his teasing, thinking what a nice man he was. Count he might be, but there wasn't an ounce of snobbishness about him. Outside the hotel he opened the door of a runaround Renault, clearly the best for nipping in and out of traffic on a working day. He took her speedily to the photographer's.

Within minutes it was all arranged. Arnaud had had similar assignments before, and knew what was expected of him. The box of photos would be delivered at the Théatre in time for distribution, and if more were required they would be dispatched to the other cities on receipt of Angela's phone call.

She had looked at the photo of Paul that morning. The fans would love it. It was a head-and-shoulders portrait of him in his customary evening jacket and white tie, the red rose in his buttonhole. It was a flattering portrait, even for Paul, and Angela's heart had leaped at her first sight of it. She was thrilled by his handsome features: the velvet brown eyes, smiling and alive with pleasure with the endearing little creases at the corners; the strong jawline and wide sensual mouth that had kissed her own with such passion and surprising tenderness; and the dark hair just long enough to be interesting, curling round his ears.

Oh yes, she thought, there would be plenty of female fans who would drool over this. Angela tried to feel amused at the idea, but the fact was, she could very easily drool over it herself.

"Paul isn't intending to sign all those photos at the stage door, is he?" Jacques asked incredulously. He drove capably through the busy streets, still colorful with tourists in mid-August. "I shouldn't think he could afford writer's cramp in *his* hands."

"No, the original one is signed across the foot of the photo, and I'm afraid the fans will have to be content with a copy of his signature."

She didn't know Paris that well yet, but surely they shouldn't be heading toward the Seine? Paul had said the recording studio was on the southern fringe of Paris. "Do you know where you're going, Jacques?"

He laughed. "I'd like to say I was abducting you, *chérie*, but I don't think Paul would be too happy about that. We have plenty of time before lunch, so I thought we'd take coffee in the Tuileries. You have heard of the garden, naturally."

She nodded. She wasn't sure Paul expected her to arrive just at lunchtime, but she was enjoying Jacques's company too much to worry. Besides, she still hoped to learn something about Paul from his friend. And the Tuileries were one part of Paris she hadn't wanted to miss. She had read about them long ago, and searched about in her memory as Jacques parked the car. They walked through the ornate gates into the vast, symmetrical garden with its fountains and flowerbeds and statues. Small tables and chairs stood under gay umbrellas at the small cafes in the center of the garden.

The Tuileries were begun by Catherine de Medici, who took up residence in the Louvre, which was then a royal palace. But it was not until early in the reign of Louis XIV that the gardens were laid out, and the Champs Élysées designed as an extension of them. Outside the gates in what was now the Place de la Concorde, the guillotine had been set up during the French Revolution.

Looking around these pleasant sunlit gardens now, with children shouting noisily as they sailed toy boats on the nearby lake, it was easy to forget that such a place was steeped in history. Angela gave a small shiver and sat down beneath one of the bright umbrellas, glad she'd been born in the twentieth century. Jacques ordered coffee and *gateaux*.

"And how are you liking your new job?" Jacques asked her. "Is Paul a hard taskmaster?"

Angela laughed. "You know him better than I do!

It's certainly an interesting job, and different from anything I've done before."

"But?"

But what? How could she tell this man that every time she and Paul clashed she felt so emotionally drained afterward she wasn't sure how she was going to last out this tour, though she didn't know how she could bear to turn her back on him, either.

"Will you tell me something about him, Jacques?" she said impulsively. "His background. Sometimes I feel I'll never get to know him properly."

The waiter brought their order to the table and she sipped the strong black coffee, eyeing the creamy *gateau*.

"We went to Oxford at the same time," Jacques told her. "That is how I know him so well, and why I speak passable English. I visited Paul's home on several occasions. He adored his mother, you know, and she was unbelievably ambitious for him. His father had died in a plane crash years before, and he'd been a concert pianist too. I don't think his mother ever got over it, and in Paul she saw the reincarnation of her husband. He certainly had plenty of talent, but it's impossible to live up to a dream, and that's what Mrs. Blake expected of him. He could never please her completely, because she demanded perfection from him; and yet she could never see the perfection that was already there. Paul's natural talent surpassed his father's, and if you think he's off on an ego trip every time he seeks to wring every bit of acclaim from his fans, I can tell you it's mainly because he wants them to recognize and appreciate the pleasure of good music as much as he does. I don't know if I'm explaining it sensibly to you, or even if you can understand what I'm saying, Angela."

She hoped she did. But she didn't care too much for the idea of such demanding parents. It was to Paul's credit that he had emerged from such a background as emotionally unscathed as he apparently had. She could understand why he would want his mother's approval of his work if he loved her so much. But she had to agree with Jacques on one thing. Paul's music reached perfection, and brought pleasure to countless people all over the world. The whims of an artistic temperament could surely be forgiven in such circumstances.

"Thank you for telling me, Jacques," she said. "It might explain one or two things, and at least I can try to be more tolerant of Paul's unpredictable moods. I suppose we should all be glad of one thing," she said with a glimmer of humor, "at least his mother didn't turn him off women!"

Jacques laughed. "I'd say not! Paul enjoys the company of women as much as any red-blooded man, myself included, which is why I was so delighted to see his new assistant. Margaret was a love, but one could hardly say she was in the bloom of youth!"

"And Claudette Dubois? She seems to be a close friend of Paul's. I only mention her because I don't want to interfere——" she said hurriedly. She was practically holding her breath until he answered.

"Oh, Paul and Claudette go back a long time, *chérie*. Some of our mutual friends wonder if they're ever going to marry. There was some talk of an engagement several years ago, but with two temperamental people and the clash of their careers—who knows? It would be a marriage of infrequent meetings." Jacques suddenly smiled, his eyes twinkling at her. "The only thing in its favor would be that every meeting would be another honeymoon, and that can't be bad!"

Angela felt her heart lurch. She didn't want to think about Paul and Claudette together, certainly not in the respect of a honeymoon. But she had to assume there was definitely more than friendship between them. She felt deflated, as if the day had suddenly cooled, and she glanced at her watch, gasping as she saw that it was nearly noon.

"Jacques, we must go. Paul will be furious——"

"Don't worry, *chérie*. The blame will be mine," he assured her, but she wasn't put at her ease by his words. The traffic was dense now, and they had the long walk through the Tuileries to reach the car. By the time they reached the recording studios it was nearer one o'clock; and as Angela had expected, Paul was pacing about in a fury.

"Where the hell have you been?" he began at once. "I phoned the hotel and they said you'd left there hours ago. I don't pay you to waste all day when I'm expecting you here. Lunch is laid on for us—unless you've already had it? That would be just typical——"

When he stopped for breath she found herself blazing at him. Jacques was still parking the car. If he'd been there, no doubt everything would have been all sweetness and light, she thought savagely. All her noble feelings toward him because of Jacques's revelations about his background swiftly vanished.

"I've been doing your work, if you must know. And then having coffee with your friend. I'm sorry if that displeases you, but we had problems getting through the traffic. I haven't had lunch and neither has Jacques. Perhaps you'd prefer it if we both left and found our own lunch?"

He stared at her coldly. "Don't be ridiculous."

He hailed a passing official and told him that Comte Vincennes would be joining them for lunch. There was no preamble, and presumably both men were of sufficient importance for the new arrangement to be dealt with smoothly. Jacques joined them a moment later, and immediately Paul seemed to relax.

"I understand you're responsible for luring my assistant away from her work," he said lightly. "No matter. Things have gone well here. We record some pieces this afternoon, but the main body of the LPs will be recorded live in concert, so it's their problem to organize mikes and so on. All you have to do, Angela, is notify the Théatre that the blokes from the studios will be setting up during my rehearsals to check for sound and acoustics, and will be present during the performances. Think you can manage that?"

"I'm sure I can," she said stiffly.

Jacques glanced at the two of them. They were as touchy as two lovers who'd just quarreled. He wondered . . .

"I'd like to take some pictures for the magazine during rehearsals, Paul." Jacques ignored the coolness between the other two. "Who's in charge?"

"Oh, if you see Armand Le Blanc, I'm sure that'll be okay. We'd better go and have lunch, or they'll be wondering what's going on here."

Angela breathed a small sigh of relief. The day's business was too important for Paul to brood for very long, and she was thankful of Jacques's presence.

After their lunch with half a dozen of the recording officials, the afternoon went smoothly. Paul had become familiar with the studio piano that morning and found it to his liking, and there were no problems with the initial recordings. She made a careful note of the pieces he played for future reference when it became time for advance publicity of the LPs, and Jacques got his pictures. They didn't get away until nearly seven o'clock, and by then all Angela wanted to do was get back to the hotel, take a shower, and go to bed. She was suddenly very tired, and last night was catching up with her.

Jacques bade them goodbye at the studios and said he'd see them sometime during the performances at the Théatre. In any case he had his complimentary tickets for the three nights, Angela told him smilingly, so they'd see him soon. She slid into the car beside Paul and he let out the clutch with a noisy crunch of the gears. He was silent for a few minutes, and she had the feeling of the calm before the storm.

"So you've decided to set your sights higher, have

you?" he snapped out at last. Angela stared at his taut face.

"What on earth are you talking about?"

"The cozy day you've spent with Jacques Vincennes, that's what I'm talking about. What ever happened to the supposedly undying love you had for your Tim character? I suppose a French count has got a lot more going for him than a mere weedy Englishman or a concert pianist!"

Angela felt her temper rise. As far as she was concerned, Paul was insufferably rude and egotistical, and now he was accusing her of being a fortune-hunter and a flirt.

"You've got a lot of nerve," she said tightly. "What I do with my life has nothing to do with you."

"Yes it has—at least while you're in my employ," he snapped back.

"And that's not likely to be very long if you go on the way you are now," she stormed. "You can find yourself another P.R.O. as soon as this tour's over anyway. I didn't take the job to be insulted every five minutes. You can take this as my notice——"

"No, I can't." He was suddenly calm. "If you're such a delicate flower that you can't take me the way I am, then you're not the girl I took you for. And I'm not generally wrong in my judgment of people."

"Naturally not." Her sarcasm was lost on him, apparently. To her surprise he put one hand over hers and gripped it tightly. Her heart was in her mouth while the car wove in and out of the evening traffic as they neared the hotel.

"I know I give you hell, Angela, and you have to admit that you give it straight back to me. We're a pair, in case you hadn't noticed." His voice suddenly hardened again. "The one thing I don't want, though, is to see you making a play for Jacques."

Of course not. She was supposed to be warding off

the groupies at the stage door, wasn't she? She'd almost forgotten that. It would hurt his image if she gave the impression of having a romance with the handsome French count. She was supposed to be *his* girl. She pushed down the thought that if only it were true she'd agree to anything he said. And what about Claudette? It was all right for Paul to keep her on his string of admirers, of course, but it seemed Angela wasn't allowed to think of anyone but the Great One! Her scathing reference to him spun into her mind. She hadn't known how true it was in his own mind!

The car stopped with a jerk at the hotel. He hadn't removed his hand from hers yet. She sat there unmoving.

"All right. I'm sorry," he said ungraciously. They were obviously words he didn't often use.

"Thank you," she said shortly. "May I get out now, please? As soon as I've had dinner I'm going to bed. I have a headache that's lasted all day——"

"You should have told me earlier. It can't have been easy for you at the recording studios. Why on earth didn't you say something?"

"It doesn't matter——" His concern took her by surprise.

"Of course it does. Take some tablets for it, Angela. I can't afford to have you getting sick."

She should have known! She got out of the car and just managed not to slam the door. The man was impossible, she raged. How could she ever have imagined she was in love with him?

Their stay in Paris progressed smoothly. Rehearsals went well, and Paul's temper wasn't quite so much in evidence. By the time the last performance began, Angela was quite familiar with the audience reaction and the excitement outside the stage door once the show was over. The groupies *were* there, she acknowledged, and she knew exactly why Charlie Cass had wanted someone young and vivacious to "ward them off," as he'd put it so crudely.

And the Paris newspapers were never slow to scent a romance, even if one wasn't necessarily there. Angela became used to being photographed with Paul—that was an accepted part of the job. But suddenly it became obvious that their names were being linked together romantically, and there was no way she could stop it, short of issuing a press statement. She had no intention of doing that. Many of the comments surrounding her and Paul were pure invention and complete nonsense. Their association was blown out of proportion in most cases. Every morning she skimmed through the latest batch of cuttings, often squirming at some of the corny headings, allied to Paul's favorite choices of music.

"Is the lovely *mademoiselle* to be Paul Blake's bride when this year's autumn leaves begin to fall? Will the concert tour end in *l'amour?*"

The flowery French phrases alternately exasperated and amused her. Occasionally they gave her a wistful pang of hope that it could all be true.

"Perhaps wedding bells will soon be sounding for the new *belle* English companion of pianist Paul," stated one paper coyly.

The cheek of some reporters! Angela fumed, wondering just how Paul was going to react to all this. Some of the comments were even more facetious.

"Paris takes the English lovers to her heart. *Vive l'amour! Vive* Paul and Angela!"

"Love's sweet music brought them together," shrieked the headlines on a woman's page article.

She still wondered about the wisdom of denying everything; but then, the reporters would seize a new ploy. The "lovers" would have had a tiff, and they'd be watched even more eagerly. It was better by far to leave things as they were. At least Paul had achieved his object, she thought bitterly. And she was the scapegoat because she couldn't deny the fact that it was sweet torment to smile into the press cameras when Paul's arm went around her at the end of each evening and she knew he smiled into her eyes for the benefit of press and public as if it really meant something.

Angela admitted freely to herself that she was in love with him, and tried to tell herself stoically that if she could get through this first ten-day stint with him, then she'd see the rest of the tour through. She could cope with anything, as long as she didn't have to cope with knowing he was in love with someone else—the glamorous Claudette Dubois, for instance. She thanked heaven that Claudette was safely away in Copenhagen with the opera.

She threw herself even more energetically into her job, knowing Paul could find no fault with her on that score. She knew she was every bit as efficient as his wonderful Margaret, and she distributed Paul's signed photos with all the aplomb of bestowing gifts to starving natives. She remembered to keep one to send to Lorna, and one to keep for herself.

As this was the last performance in Paris, Angela relaxed. She had done a good job, and Paul could have no complaints. She had smoothed the way for him, which was more than could be said for his effect on *her*, she thought ruefully. But she wasn't going to let any such thoughts mar the enjoyment of this last concert.

She waited in the wings, listening to the music she was beginning to know so well. Everything had gone like clockwork, and the recording boys had done a splendid job all through. They were quite unobtrusive, and as she listened to Paul's rich voice giving his little introduction to each piece, in both English and French, her eyes roved around the beautiful theater, scented now with the last of the summer roses and one great display of autumn foliage on stage.

". . . and this piece is by Frédéric Chopin; Paris

became the center of his life. Chopin's father was French, though Polish by adoption. Frédéric Chopin was an elegant young man who died still in his prime at the age of thirty-nine. He enjoyed intimate, aristocratic gatherings. Tonight I give you a typical offering of the romantic music of Chopin. The 'Nocturne in E Flat,' known by several other titles. Here then is 'Tristesse'— 'So Deep Is the Night.'"

He knew exactly how to appeal to the audience, Angela reflected. Her admiration for him as a showman was intense, and to her ears he was a perfectionist at the piano. In the wings, she was directly in line with him as he sat at the beautiful grand piano, the spotlight illuminating him. He gave no sign that he was aware of her, or of anything else but the music. He gave himself to it utterly, alternating, as he so often did, between the classical version of a piece and its popular interpretation. His touch was exquisite. She joined in the applause at the end of the Chopin, knowing the audience would rise to the next, the glorious Liszt composition, "Hungarian Rhapsody No. 2," which was one of Paul's particular favorites.

When the applause for it died away, her heart gave a little leap of anticipation. The program had varied each evening, but Paul had finished each performance with his version of "Autumn Leaves." Each time she heard it, Angela's memory flew back to that evening in the hotel room when she had nearly given in to his seduction. She still half regretted the instinct that had made her flee from something she had wanted as badly as Paul.

She realized his little spiel was different this evening, and that as he spoke his eyes flickered toward her instead of being directed solely at the audience. And being Parisians, they sensed a romance and applauded even before the piece began.

". . . some of you know that one of my favorite pieces of music is the well-known 'Autumn Leaves.' I wonder if you knew it started life here in France in 1947. Its original title was *'Les Feuilles Mortes,'* with music by Joseph Kosma and French lyrics by Jacques Prévert. In my country it became famous when Johnny Mercer wrote the words to the familiar English version that has been recorded by so many great singers. It has a special meaning for me, because it has become something of a trademark, and lately because it is a favorite of a very special lady in my life. If you will allow me tonight, I would like to dedicate this final item on the program to her. To my lady with hair the color of autumn leaves."

Angela felt the prickling starting in her neck as he looked straight into her eyes. She didn't know whether to love him or hate him for doing this to her. He was as good as telling the world they were having an affair. Part of her desperately longed to believe he was sincere in saying she was special in his life, but the practical part of her told her it was all for publicity and nothing more. It was good for his image. The prickling seemed to be centering in her eyes now. They blurred slightly as the lovely strains of Paul's music filled the vast hall, accompanied this time by the theater's own small orchestra, muted in the background so as not to detract from the pianist.

She saw the smile on his lips as he looked her way, acknowledging her presence. She heard the rippling liquid notes that were so magical from his fingertips and was captivated by them as she always was. She couldn't help it. For the length of time it took to play the piece, Angela knew she was utterly and totally his, transported in her mind to that hotel room where they'd danced almost motionless in each other's arms. The audience didn't exist. There were only the two of them in that vast hall, his eyes meeting hers across the distance of the stage, and she knew with certainty that he was reliving it too.

111

Chapter Seven

The party at the end of the Paris tour was almost a letdown. From the management's viewpoint it was a triumph, of course. The concerts had been sold out and Paul's popularity had shot up. Anyone who was anyone was at the party, and the guest list included press and aristocracy, city dignitaries and showbiz personalities who were in town. The press had a ball, and Angela was the object of much curiosity—no doubt comparing the girl with hair the color of autumn leaves with the ice-cold beauty of Claudette Dubois, she thought cynically.

There was no doubt the papers were going to be full of it the next morning, and Paul's triumphant grin every time he looked her way told her he thought it a bit of inspiration on his part. Angela thought differently. Even Jacques seemed surprised. He managed to confront her in a corner of the crush of people.

"I've never seen Paul get so personal on stage before," he told her. "Did you know this was going to happen, Angela?"

"No, I didn't!" Her voice sounded a little shaky. "I don't know what it will do for his image, but I'm more concerned with what it does to mine!"

He squeezed her shoulder, his arm around her affectionately.

"It will do wonders, *chérie*. All of Paris loves a lover, and the notion that it may have happened right under

112

their noses in their own city of romance only enhances it for them."

"I was thinking more about England than Paris," she commented. "And besides, *nothing's* happened. That's what I mean. It's all a fantasy!"

"And you wish something had?" Jacques whispered knowingly. He put a light kiss on her cheek. *"Ma pauvre* Angela. Don't let the misery show! Tonight is supposed to be a joyful one."

She blushed furiously at letting the naked emotions show so easily. So Jacques was aware of the way she felt. She saw Paul making his way toward them, and because she knew his moods so well, she slid out of Jacques's friendly embrace.

"Come and meet M. de Bray, darling. He won't believe me when I tell him we've only known each other a few weeks. And they say the French are the romantic ones! I thought they'd have known all about love at first sight!"

She stared at him. The words were romantic, destined for any stray reporter's ears nearby, but she was aware of the barbed tone, and knew very well he hadn't approved of seeing her with Jacques's arm around her. His own arm replaced it, and his lips nuzzled into her neck. She suddenly capitulated. Why he was playing this game she didn't know, but two could play as well as one, perhaps even better!

She shook hands with the portly little man and laughed up into Paul's eyes adoringly. It didn't take too much pretence.

"Oh, I wouldn't say it was quite love at first sight, M. de Bray. Maybe at second sight. Wouldn't you say so, darling?"

Paul was startled by her reaction, but he hid it well. He suddenly started to enjoy himself, including Angela in all his conversation as he circulated round the room. To everyone, they appeared as two people wanting to be together, two people in love. It was inevitable that some of the reporters should ask if there was going to be an announcement made during the French tour. Angela managed to press her foot against Paul's at that moment. Surely he wouldn't dare go that far.

"You'll have to wait and see." She heard him laugh. "You must allow us some privacy. But if there's anything to tell, I'm sure my personal assistant will be pleased to let you in on it."

He made it sound as if she was a *very* personal assistant. Just how would he have acted this evening if Claudette had been here? Angela wondered, with a stab of anger. Would she have been the one to be sharing all this attention instead of herself? If it was all a cheap publicity stunt, which of course it was, she didn't think much of it. The whole charade was beginning to depress her. She whispered to Paul that she hoped this party wouldn't go on all night. He squeezed her closer to his side as he whispered back that he hoped not either. She ignored the meaning he conveyed that he'd rather have her to himself. She had no intention of continuing the playacting when they were alone. If she didn't hold on tightly to her self-control, she would end up in tears, and that would be unthinkable, and very bad for Paul's public image.

At last it was all over, and they were ushered to the car as if they were royalty. By then the press people had assured Angela they'd arrange for the news items and pictures to be syndicated to England for the English papers. Jacques had said he'd meet them in Orléans if he could make it; otherwise he'd see them in Cannes for sure. Some merry Frenchmen had whipped the red rose from Paul's buttonhole and fastened it to Angela's shoulder, and the fragrance of it drifted up to her nostrils as she sank down exhausted beside him in the car. But she wasn't too exhausted to let her feelings out.

"You must be mad," she said baldly. "And I must be

mad to let you get away with it! What on earth made you do it?"

"Is it so objectionable to you?" he countered.

Angela was taken aback for a minute. "It's impossible! Do you really expect me to go round the country pretending to be your—your—well, whatever you had in mind! I dread to think what those French reporters are going to make of it. And you realize it'll be in the English papers as well? What do you think Tim is going to think when he sees it?" Her anger was increasing every minute.

"Is his opinion still so important to you?" Paul demanded. "As far as I know, you haven't telephoned him, or even sent him a postcard since we've been here. Is that really the way a girl in love behaves? Don't throw Tim at me, Angela!"

He was absolutely right, but the fact that he knew it didn't improve her temper. She was already guilty enough about not writing or phoning either Tim or Lorna. There hadn't been time, so she pushed them out of her mind. There were more immediate things to concentrate on.

"I still don't see why you had to give people the impression that ours is more than a business arrangement," she said angrily.

"Because you and I both know that it is," he said calmly.

"And what do you think Mlle. Dubois will make of it when she reads the papers?" Angela burst out.

"Claudette is a very dear friend, and I'm sure she'll want only my happiness."

"Precisely," Angela muttered. "She'll want your happiness as long as it includes her!"

"Are you jealous?"

Angela began to laugh. It was high-pitched and she swallowed hard. "No, I'm not——"

"Because perhaps we had better make it official, to avoid any misunderstandings. An engagement isn't binding, Angela. It can always be broken, but if it makes you feel more secure——"

This wasn't real, she told herself. Here they were, speeding through the empty streets in the early hours, calmly talking about a mockery of an engagement. *Why?* It didn't make sense. Unless with that ego of Paul's, when some pressman had made an arch comment about his attractive companion, perhaps he hadn't been able to resist telling him they were lovers? And with his abhorrence of rejection, he was prepared to go to these lengths.

He obviously didn't believe in the sanctity of marriage, she thought bitterly. It surprised her. With someone of Paul's sensitivity, she'd have expected something more of him. Though hadn't he once said that he had no intention of getting caught up in that trap? So an engagement, if she agreed to it, was obviously all a sham. It would mean nothing, and there would be no happy ending.

Why was she even considering it? she asked herself furiously. It was insulting of him to suggest it for the sake of giving an extra air of glamor to his tour.

The fact was, she *was* considering it, for the simple reason she just couldn't ignore it. Nor could she escape the fact that if it had been meant sincerely, with love behind every word, she'd be delirious with joy right this minute. She'd never been a girl who was satisfied with second best. It was why she'd never have been able to marry Tim. But what Paul was suggesting now— pretending to be his fiancée—would be the next best thing to reality.

Angela hated herself for weakening. It wasn't in her nature. She'd always been so strong, but in Paul she'd met a will stronger than her own. It was what drew them together . . . that, the love on her part, and something more basic on his.

The car drew up outside the hotel. Only the foyer

was dimly lit at this hour. Paul demanded an answer aggressively. It was hardly the manner of a lover, and a glimmer of amusement lightened her mood. Paul suddenly caught her hands in his, and his face was very near to her own. In the confines of the car, she was desperately aware of his physical attractions.

"Well, Angela?" he spoke softly, his mouth gentle as he changed his tactics. "Do we crown this successful Paris tour by announcing our engagement, no matter how temporary? Call it an engagement of convenience if you like! Less pressure on me from my ever-loving fans and the newshounds who never let up in search of a romance, and a bit of prestige for you, if you choose to look at it that way. Unless of course, you're saving yourself for something better. If the idea of being a countess is making you hesitate, I'll quite understand."

"No, it's not," she said angrily.

"Well then! Or are you afraid of committing yourself? I give you my word you can call the whole thing off any time you wish, and I'll do the gentlemanly thing and hide behind a broken heart for a few weeks!" His tone was mocking again.

All right, blast him! If he thought he was so desirable a catch and wanted to take part in this charade, all right!

"I agree." She said it quickly, before she could change her mind.

She'd half expected him to pull her into his arms and rain kisses on her lips. Instead, he moved away from her and got out of the car, opening her door for her as politely as any chauffeur.

"Good," he said briefly. "I shan't expect you to be in touch with the press about this, of course. I'll see to it myself."

Angela opened her mouth to object, suddenly struck by nerves. But how could she object? She'd just agreed to the mock engagement, and a man in Paul's position would expect to find a mention of it in the newspapers. The magnitude of what she'd done by agreeing hadn't fully gotten through to her yet.

Apparently Paul intended to phone the press that minute, to catch the same editions that would be reporting his last performance. And knowing the French reporters, they'd love the romantic little reference he'd made to his "lady with hair the color of autumn leaves." There'd be no doubt now who he meant, and Claudette would be livid.

"Would you mind if I go on to bed?" She was suddenly so weary she couldn't be bothered to think any more. "I need my beauty sleep before the drive to Orléans tomorrow."

Paul nodded, without any reference to her remark. She might have expected him to say she didn't need beauty sleep, but his mind was obviously on other things. He didn't need to chat her up any longer, she thought bitterly. Not that he'd ever been too subtle about that anyway.

She went into her own room. After the excitement of the concert and the party was over, and the extraordinary outcome afterward, Angela felt almost numb with shock. She was engaged to Paul Blake. Not in any romantic sense, but in the eyes of the world she was the girl he was going to marry. They'd expect to see them happy together, like any young couple in love.

A sudden surge of longing swept through her, and she closed her eyes briefly. If only it were true. If only Paul really loved her, she would be the happiest girl on earth now, instead of feeling such a hollow emptiness inside her. Salt tears stung her eyelids, because this wasn't the way she'd expected her betrothal to be. She'd always vowed she would wait for the right man. Well, he'd come along all right, she knew, but he didn't seem to know she existed, except for his convenience.

She was just slipping into bed when there was a tap

on her door. She didn't answer. It had to be Paul, and she just couldn't take any more tonight.

"If you don't open this door, I'll alert the night porter that I think you're ill," his voice came pleasantly through the door, calm but insistent. "I'll get another key easily enough, and I won't keep you more than a moment, I promise."

She didn't believe him, but neither did she want any gawking hotel staff gossiping about the fact that M. Blake had insisted on going into her room at this hour. Angela threw on a dressing gown and opened the door an inch. He stood there immobile until she sighed and stood back from it.

She was like a small defensive fawn, Paul found himself thinking. Her arms were wrapped round her delicious little body as she looked up at him defiantly. Her face was devoid of makeup now, her hair a soft golden halo where she'd brushed it out. A rush of tenderness for her engulfed him at her vulnerable, childlike appearance—an impression that was in complete opposition to her womanly shape. She exasperated him by her resistance to him. He amazed himself that he put up with it. With any other woman he'd have been seeking his pleasures elsewhere by now, instead of taking a weird delight in practically forcing her into this engagement. Even now, he wasn't fully sure himself why he had suggested it—unless she was right in her taunts, and he was just too egotistical to believe she could really be unmoved by him. He squashed the thought immediately and held out a little square box to her.

"What's this?" she said suspiciously.

Paul opened the box, and she gasped. Inside was an exquisite antique ring; emeralds set in a Victorian circlet. It was obviously worth a good deal of money.

"I wanted you to have this. We have to make the show plausible, don't we? It was my mother's ring."

Angela stared at it. Her throat felt thick.

"I—I can't——" she stammered.

Paul ignored her protest. With one movement he took the ring from its box and slipped it on her engagement finger. They both looked at it for a long moment as it glittered there. It was slightly loose, but not loose enough for her to lose it. He suddenly bent his head and lifted her hand to his lips, kissing both the ring and her finger. And then he touched her lips very gently with his.

"Now we've sealed the bargain with a loving kiss," he said softly. "That will be enough—for now. Good-night, Angela, my angel."

He turned and left her, closing the door behind him. The ring felt cold and unfamiliar on her finger. Angela's eyes blurred with tears as she traced its contours with her forefinger. She got back into bed, burying her head under the sheets before the tears became a torrent. She'd been a crazy fool ever to agree to this, and Paul's words only made the deception seem more shameful.

She presented herself at his door before breakfast the next morning. She'd hardly slept, and only the skillful use of makeup hid the shadows beneath her lovely hazel eyes. Otherwise, no one seeing her would have taken her for the happy engaged girl she was supposed to be.

His eyes went at once to her left hand, and she gave him a twisted smile.

"Yes, I'm wearing it, Paul," she said flatly. "Since the papers will have the news by now, I can hardly back down, can I? But I want you to understand that I'll only carry on the charade in public. When we're alone it's to be business as usual. You're my boss and I'm your assistant, and nothing more. I can't stand—I can't stand you touching me——" her voice faltered. If she went on any more, she'd be telling him she couldn't bear the pretense of it when she wanted so badly for it to be real.

Paul completely misunderstood her meaning. He took the words at face value, his face hard and angry.

"I see. Thank you for telling me so bluntly. No doubt the pleasure of wearing a valuable ring and the adulation you receive as my fiancée will help you overcome your repugnance of me for a few weeks at least. Once we get back to England we can let the excitement die down and in due course issue a small statement to the press to the effect that the marriage will not take place. I believe that's the official wording. Will that suit you, *chérie?*"

He was hurtfully insulting, but Angela refused to allow it to upset her. At all costs she intended to retain her dignity. She thanked him quietly and told him she was all packed and ready to leave as soon as they'd had breakfast, if that was what he wished. He'd never guess how her stomach was churning when he'd said "the marriage will not take place." It never would have, of course, but his cold words seemed to be the death knell to all her dreams.

They went down to the hotel dining room in total silence; but once there, Angela saw at once that the staff had got wind of the supposed romance that had blossomed right under their noses. They were charmed by it, and on their table was a bowl of red roses as a small tribute to them both. Paul the showman took over.

He replied for both of them as congratulations poured in. Somehow Angela smiled and sparkled and showed her ring for the envious waitress who asked to see it. Inevitably a reporter had arrived from somewhere to get the first interview with the newly engaged couple over breakfast. Angela could just guess how the wording of that was going to look. A call came through for Paul from Charlie Cass, and when he said Charlie wanted to talk to her as well, she realized the news had reached the English papers very quickly.

"Well, this is a surprise, Angela!" His voice was smarmy over the line. "I thought you and Paul were going to get along, despite the 'off,' but I didn't think it would move this fast!"

Her cheeks burned at the implication that she'd known exactly what she was doing by taking on the P.R.O. job.

"Neither did I, Charlie," she said coolly. "But you know what they say about Paris being the city for lovers, don't you?"

She heard his knowing chuckle. It wasn't quite what she'd meant to say, particularly when Paul was grinning beside her, fully aware of her embarrassment.

"Everything's going well, I take it? Apart from you and Paul, I mean. You're all set for Orléans this morning. Hotel booked okay?"

"All taken care of, Charlie. I'll be in touch if we hit any problems. Do you want to talk to Paul again?"

"No need, sweetheart. Oh—make sure there are plenty of those fan photos available for the rest of the tour. Those French mamselles will be drooling over Paul even more now they know he's officially out of reach."

Angela put the phone down with a bang. Paul wouldn't have told Charlie the truth about their engagement, she was sure, but his tone suggested that he believed it was either a clever publicity stunt on Paul's behalf, or that she was a fast-moving gold digger. Either way, it didn't make her feel comfortable.

"Smile, darling," Paul breathed in her ear. "Jacques has just turned up."

She wasn't going to fool him, Angela thought desperately. He knew Paul too well and he was too aware of how they antagonized each other; but after a searching look in her eyes he told Paul he was the luckiest fellow alive.

Jacques kissed her soundly. "People like you are food and drink to a dreary reporter's life," he said enthusiastically. "Just a couple more pictures, and then I'll let you get on your way, Paul. I couldn't miss out on a breakfast shot of the happy couple."

Paul's hand squeezed hers under cover of the table-cloth, and she smiled brightly into Jacques's camera, her left hand placed over Paul's so that the ring glittered between them.

Just before they left the hotel there was another phone call. It was Claudette calling from Copenhagen. The last thing Angela wanted was to speak to her, but Paul said she had asked specifically to have a few words with Angela. Her heart was thudding as she took the receiver.

"Congratulations, darling." Claudette's voice was brittle with sarcasm. "I underestimated you! I wonder just what magic you managed to work to turn Paul's mind to marriage when everybody knows he likes his women unattached? I don't see him settling down with the little earth mother somehow."

Angela gasped. Claudette was clearly incensed at the news, wanting Paul for herself. Angela had known that all along, even if Paul hadn't. She thanked Claudette as coolly as possible for her "good wishes," trying not to betray the anger she felt at her insults. Claudette laughed maliciously.

"You haven't won yet, my dear." Her voice dropped to a thin sneer. "And we Frenchwomen don't give up that easily. I look forward to seeing you again at the Château Vincennes. We'll see then who is capable of holding M. Paul Blake's heart!"

The line went dead, and Angela swallowed involuntarily. The words had been as vindictive as a threat. She wondered what Paul's reaction would be if he knew that Claudette saw her as a rival now, and intended to put all her charms to work at Jacques's house party to take him from her. No doubt it would amuse him to think there were two women fighting over him. At the very least it would gratify his ego, so she certainly had no intention of telling him.

Anyway, she amended hastily, *she* wasn't going to give Claudette the satisfaction of fighting with her over anyone. By the time they reached the château in the Camargue, the tour would be over, and the charade could come to an end. If it was obvious by then that the two of them were cooling off, so much the better. Claudette was welcome to him. It was better to keep her feelings hardened against him than to let the soft warm emotions take her over and admit to herself how much she loved him, and how jittery the opera singer was making her.

At last they were on their way out of Paris and driving south on the road to Orléans. Once there, Angela was sure the rush of showbiz excitement that had surrounded them in Paris would be less intense. They knew Paul in Paris. He'd been there often before, whereas this tour of the other cities was by way of a new experience for him as well as for Angela. She gave a deep sigh and settled down in the passenger seat.

"Do you think you'll be able to cope?" Paul said evenly. "I'm sorry about this morning. I thought we'd be able to slip out of the hotel without any fuss."

She hadn't been as edgy about the fuss as the phone call from Claudette. And she couldn't hide it from him any longer.

"Your girlfriend wasn't pleased," she burst out.

"What girlfriend?" He scowled at a French driver who passed too close to their car and gave him a blast of horn. "*You're* my girlfriend, remember?"

His words didn't give her the glow they should have.

"I'm talking about Claudette, of course," she snapped. "You must be blind if you don't realize she's dying to be Mrs. Paul Blake!"

He glanced at her. Her face was flushed, but he wasn't sure if it was from emotion or anger.

"You needn't worry on Claudette's account," he said coldly. "She and I have a long understanding, and if she said anything to upset you, which I'm sure wouldn't have been intentional, then it's merely the passionate Frenchwoman in her. She'll be as sweet as honey the next time you meet her."

He really believed it, Angela thought incredulously. He really thought the beautiful Claudette was going to be pleased at his engagement to another woman. A woman like her didn't let go once she'd gotten her hooks into a man, and the "long understanding" obviously meant more to her than to him. Claudette was too possessive to let him go to a girl who'd known him only a few weeks. Her ego was as fragile as Paul's in that respect, and she'd see it as the biggest slight of all time. Angela shivered, thankful at least that the house party was still some time away. Maybe Claudette's wrath would have cooled down a little in that time.

She was able to think more rationally by the time they reached the old city of Orléans, with its lovely cathedral, its wide, winding river and elegant squares. The hotel was older than the one in Paris, and as Paul had predicted, they were greeted with no more curiosity than was normally accorded to English VIPs. The rooms they were given were adjoining, but Paul made no comment on that fact, to her relief. It was mid-afternoon by the time they had settled in and unpacked. The procedure Angela had gone through in Paris to make Paul's tour run smoothly didn't have to be started until tomorrow; and anyway, now that she knew the ropes, she viewed it with more confidence.

When she had changed into something cooler after a quick shower, she picked up the phone and asked the hotel receptionist to get the number of her old flat in England. She had to let Lorna know she was all right before her flatmate wondered if she'd been abducted. Besides, she wanted to know if the news of her "engagement" had reached Lorna and Tim yet.

As an afterthought she asked the girl at the desk to send her up some iced lemonade. It was a hot afternoon and there was no air conditioning in the hotel. The breeze blowing in through the window hardly stirred the warm air. Though the hotel was old, some of the large rooms had been made into two by partition walls, and they weren't entirely sound-proofed. She could hear small movements from Paul's room next door: the creak of the bed, the scrape of a chair, the opening of his window.

The phone in her room shrilled out, and when she picked it up she heard the sound of Lorna's familiar voice saying their number. A sudden wave of homesickness took Angela by surprise, so that she didn't speak for a few seconds, and then the words came out in a little rush.

"Lorna, it's me—Angela. I'm sorry I haven't rung you before, but things have been so hectic here."

"Hectic! Is that what you call it?" Lorna's voice was full of cautious excitement. "You're a dark horse, aren't you, Angie? All those things you said about Paul Blake, and now you're going to *marry* him! I hope you're going to tell me every single detail of how it happened—only not right now."

So the English papers had got hold of the story as quickly as she'd expected. Angela groaned. But there had been something odd in Lorna's voice.

"Is everything all right?" she said quickly. "You don't sound quite yourself——"

"Oh, heck." There was a muffled sound at the other end as if Lorna had put her hand over the receiver a moment. Then her voice came back. "Angela, Tim's here. He's upset, and he wants to talk to you."

"Oh no——" But it was too late. She was forced to listen to Tim's imploring voice telling her she'd rushed into this engagement too fast; that she should take time to think it over; that he still loved her; and what a shock it had been to see the news in the paper that morning without any warning from her. He was hurt, and he showed it. Angela felt hunted, but telling him it was all a sham would only make things worse. He'd only think there was still hope for him, and she knew quite certainly that there wasn't. And guiltily, she knew his impassioned words were making her impatient with him. Why couldn't he ever take no for an answer?

"Tim, please listen to me. I don't want you to feel badly about this," she said edgily. "But be honest. I told you a dozen times that I couldn't marry you, didn't I? I do care about you though——"

"You've got a fine way of showing it, by getting engaged to somebody else!" He sounded petulant, and Angela had to steel herself not to slam the phone down. She'd had about enough of temperamental males lately. "You didn't take so long to accept this Blake guy. I suppose he had more glamor than I did, is that it? I wasn't famous enough for you. I never expected it of you, Angie."

She counted to ten. She didn't want to quarrel with Tim, but he was pushing her toward it very fast.

"You know me well enough to know I don't care about glamor," she snapped. "Why won't you be sensible about this, and try to understand it has nothing whatever to do with you and me? We were over long before I took this job."

He didn't seem to be listening to her at all. He spoke bitterly.

"I wonder if you ever cared for me at all, Angela!"

"Of course I cared for you. I still do——" As a friend! Why the blazes couldn't he settle for that?

The click of the door didn't worry her. It would be the maid with the iced lemonade. But she was tired of arguing on the phone like this. She wasn't going to get anywhere while Tim was in this mournful mood.

"Look, Tim, I'll explain it all in a letter. It'll only upset us both to go on like this," she said evenly.

There was a movement behind her. She whirled round, still holding the phone. Instead of the maid, Paul stood inside the door, his arms folded, a look of controlled fury on his face. She mumbled a quick goodbye into the phone, slamming it back on its rest, and faced Paul with a pounding heart.

"And just what are you going to explain to darling Tim?" he said explosively. "Do you intend to keep him dangling on the hook as well as me? Or has he already sampled the delights you pretend to keep to yourself, my *darling?* I'm beginning to think I'm being a fool to treat you like porcelain. Perhaps this is the treatment you prefer, for all that you pretend otherwise!"

He strode across to her and pulled her roughly into his arms, pressing his mouth on hers in a savage kiss. His hand sought the softness of her breasts beneath the thin tee shirt she wore, and felt their quick response to his caress. The suddenness of his approach startled her, so that before she could stop herself she was kissing him back, wildly and passionately. She wanted his touch, his caresses, his warmth and his passion. She wanted him more than anything else on earth at that moment. A wild excitement was rushing through her veins as she felt his rapid heartbeats against hers and the hard rousing of his passion. She was dizzy with longing for him when the insistent tapping on her door made her push away from him with a gasp.

The maid entered with the iced lemonade, looking modestly away from the two English guests. What they did was no concern of hers, but she wondered afterward why the gentleman muttered a sudden oath and strode out of the room and down to the bar, leaving the pretty young lady with such a look of unfulfillment in her eyes and her cheeks flushed.

Chapter Eight

Dinner that evening was a stilted affair. The conversation was brief, only softening when any of the hotel staff was nearby. Angela was consumed with misery and anger. Paul's quick changes of mood were beginning to be more than she could take. And his arrogant reaction to her phone call with Tim was quite unnecessary.

Of course, she knew how it looked to him. She'd mentioned that she was going to phone her flatmate, and when Paul had come into her room so unobtrusively she was speaking to Tim and calling him darling and protesting that she still cared for him. She could have explained how it happened, but why should she? She was still bristling all over at his high-handed treatment of her, and he could think what he liked. If he chose to think she really was still in love with Tim and intending to marry him eventually, Angela had no intention of disillusioning him.

"I don't think you'll be wanting my company this evening." He looked at her coldly across the dinner table. "I'm sure you can amuse yourself, and I'll see you in the morning. *Au revoir, chérie.*"

He bent and kissed her swiftly, his hand pressing hers as he spoke the final words more intimately. All for the benefit of the starry-eyed waitress who was hovering nearby to clear away their table, Angela thought cynically. She watched his tall rangy figure disappear from the dining room and could have wept. He was a fool, for all his sophistication, she stormed inside. Couldn't he see she loved him? Her common sense asserted itself. Thank heaven he couldn't. It was the one trump card she held in this little game of his. Once he suspected she wasn't as immune to him as she tried to appear, he'd put on all the charm of which he was capable, and she didn't know how much longer she'd be able to hold out against it. Remembering the night in Paris, with his music playing softly on the cassette player in his bedroom and the way he had edged her toward the bed with soft words and tingling kisses, Angela no longer trusted her own feelings.

She needed a breath of air. She had no idea where Paul had gone, but she fetched a thin jacket to cover her sleeveless dress and left the old hotel to stroll along the banks of the river. It was cooler there, away from the city traffic, its tree-lined banks giving a little shade. Lovers with their arms entwined took advantage of the gnarled tree trunks to pause and kiss, and their presence only made Angela feel more alone. She watched an old barge move slowly upriver for a while and then turned her footsteps back to the hotel. No matter how beautiful the surroundings, they were enhanced by sharing them. She remembered Paul saying as much, and tried to push him out of her thoughts.

Back in her hotel room she started to write to Tim and Lorna, though it proved more difficult than she expected. How could she explain her reasons for this sudden engagement to Tim, who'd loved her so patiently for so long, and believed sincerely that he'd win her in the end?

He sounded so dull, Angela thought guiltily. He *was* dull, compared with someone like—like Paul, or Jacques Vincennes. It wasn't Tim's fault. It was just the way he was. Some other girl would find him exciting and wonderful, and he'd obviously make a marvelous husband and father, but not for Angela.

She sighed, crushing the first piece of paper in her hand and throwing it in the wastebasket. Her instincts had been to tell Tim and Lorna the truth, but she realized that she couldn't do that. It wouldn't be fair to Paul. If news leaked out that the engagement was all a gimmick, it would damage his image, and she couldn't do that to him. Neither Tim nor Lorna would dream of betraying her confidence, but an innocent word in the wrong place might stir up a hornet's nest.

In the end she knew she'd just have to write a gentle, friendly letter to Tim and hope he wouldn't hate her. Knowing his soft heart, she knew that appealing to him in that way would result in a generous wish for her happiness, with no more reference to his broken heart. Angela felt guilty all over again, but it was the only thing to do, and she did it.

To Lorna, she wrote very differently. As far as her friend was concerned, Angela had found the love of a lifetime, a love that was all the more spectacular because she had been initially so unimpressed by the thought of working for Paul. Writing to Lorna, she could at least tell the truth about her own feelings for the man. She could pretend for a while that she really was going to be the future Mrs. Paul Blake. Her heart skipped a beat as the words came into her head:

> I know you think I must be crazy, Lorna, but if love ever hits you the way it hit me, you'll know it's useless to fight it. I love Paul so much. He's the first thing I think about when I wake each morning, and he's my last thought when I go to sleep at night. And all the hours between when we're together, I wonder how I ever existed before he came into my life.

Angela read over the words she'd written. She tried to see them logically, as if she was Lorna reading them. Yes, they'd convey the impression of a newly engaged girl, deliriously in love. . . . Who was she kidding? she asked herself tremblingly. They were a true reflection of her own feelings. For once she was writing from the heart instead of hiding behind the mask of pretense, and for once it didn't matter. It was what Lorna would expect to hear, and it was a blessed relief not to keep her emotions bottled up inside herself.

Don't start asking me when the wedding's going to be. Life's too hectic for us to think about it yet, and besides, we need to get to know each other properly. But I'm wildly happy, and the only thing that clouds my happiness a little is poor Tim. Lord knows I told him often enough that I wasn't going to marry him, but I know he's the sort who never gives up hope. If you see him, Lorna, try to make him understand that it would never have worked for us. He needs a bit of company right now . . .

She hoped that didn't sound as if she was trying to throw Lorna and Tim together, because that wouldn't work either! Before she started sounding too much like a matchmaker, Angela decided she'd better finish the letter.

If you want to write back, you can send it to the Château Vincennes near Arles. Paul and I will be there for a week at the end of the tour, and knowing you it'll be at least a month before you get around to writing. We're going there as guests of Comte Vincennes, who's a real darling. I suppose you could say I'm moving in some exalted circles, especially as Claudette Dubois will be there too. She's an opera singer, famous in France and plenty of other places, but I know with your musical tastes you won't recognize the name! Anyway, Lorna, I'd love to hear from you when you feel like writing.

When she'd signed the letter Angela reread it. Her mouth twisted. Most of it was true, except that there wasn't going to be any wedding and she wasn't wildly happy. She suddenly leaned her head on her arms on the little writing desk in her room and felt the weak tears squeeze through. For a girl who rarely cried, she seemed to be doing more than her fair share over Paul, she thought shakily.

There was a TV set in her room and she turned it on, keeping the volume low. She didn't really want to watch, but it would keep her thoughts from straying to Paul, as they usually did. She tried to feel amused at the American film she'd seen several times already, appallingly dubbed with French voices.

At about ten o'clock she rang for room service to bring her some coffee, and afterward she went to bed. But she couldn't sleep. She wished she hadn't mentioned Claudette in her letter to Lorna, because it brought her vindictive voice instantly to mind.

"You haven't won yet, my dear . . . and we French-women don't give up that easily."

Angela shivered. This whole thing, the engagement, the sudden fervor of the French press at scenting a romance, and the fury of Claudette Dubois had suddenly turned the whole affair into a duel between the two of them. The speed of it all was bewildering enough, without the added distaste of the deception, and the knowledge that she'd made a sure enemy in Claudette.

She moved restlessly in the large double bed. Moonlight filtered through the lace curtains at the windows, throwing patterns across the wallpaper as they shifted in the soft breeze. The city around the hotel was quietening now, and she wondered where Paul was and what he was doing. As if in answer, she heard his door open and close a short while later, and the soft movements as he prepared for bed. The bed in his room must be against the same wall as hers, she thought instantly, and she heard the creak of his as he slid under the covers.

She lay there sleepless, hardly daring to move, not wanting him to be aware that she was still awake. But she was very aware of him. So close . . . there was barely an inch of wall between them. She tried not to picture him there, but it was impossible to put the image away from her. His dark head indenting the pillow, his strong handsome face turned toward the window, perhaps watching the same patterned moonlight. It gave her an oddly sensual feeling to think they shared the same view. Apart and yet together.

Angela felt a surge of longing. She loved him and everything in her cried out for them to be together at that moment, if only Paul loved her in return, if only his desire for her wasn't merely to satisfy his own ego. Even if he'd pretend, for just a little while, she would give in to him. He was willing to pretend to the world that he wanted to make her his wife, but in private he couldn't even be subtle enough to pretend he loved her.

The rush of emotion began to die down, to her relief. Thank God he *didn't* pretend, she told herself passionately. Because if he ever did, she'd be lost.

The next day Angela discovered that Paul had taken her phone call with Tim very much to heart. There wasn't the same adulation for him here as in Paris, and from now on the tour would be less frenetic. There was no need to be quite so adoring toward each other in public, he told her coldly, and in private she could spend all day on the phone to England if she chose, as long as she saw that all went smoothly for him.

Her eyes smarted at his tone. She was tired of protesting that her life was her own, and it would suit her purposes for him to think she was still in love with Tim, so she let the jibes pass.

From then on the job took over. She concentrated on doing just as he asked: making it all run smoothly for him, ignoring his moods as much as possible, smiling into the cameras with him when occasion and the press demanded it, and acknowledging in public that she was his fiancée. She tried not to let the wild, sweet longings overcome her when the end of every performance was preceded by Paul's now expected comments about the lady in his life, and then the familiar strains of "Autumn Leaves" that could tug at her heart.

She wished sometimes there could have been a third party with them, and hoped Jacques would join them as a buffer. But a telegram arrived to say he was unavoidably detained in Paris for several more weeks. He wished Paul luck in his concerts, sent his love to Angela and said he'd see them in Cannes.

The tour was a success, there was no doubt of that. Paul's music enchanted the romantic French, and Angela admitted there were as many stage-door groupies as Charlie Cass had predicted. They clamored for the give-away photos of Paul, and waited eagerly for him to toss his red rose into the crowd with as many screams of delight as if he was a pop star.

Everywhere they went it was the same. Angela saw that the advance publicity reached the local papers before the performances, and always there was some snippet about her own presence. Somehow every newspaperman had latched onto that, whether she was asked about it or not. All the world loves a lover, she thought cynically, and the French in particular.

All the same, it was Paul's talent that really drew the crowds. She despised his arrogance even though she loved him, but she could do nothing other than respect his dedication to his profession. He never tired of smiling to his fans or pausing to sign autographs. He never stopped rehearsing until he had perfection at his fingertips. His mother could have been justly proud of him, Angela found herself thinking time and again when she listened in the wings of a theater to the pure magic of his music that held his audience spellbound.

Orléans . . . Nantes . . . the beautiful wine country of Bordeaux . . . Lyons . . . and finally Cannes. It was the last stop before the final concerts in Marseille, and then the week of relaxation at the Château Vincennes. They would need it, Angela knew. It had been more strenuous than she had expected, and if she felt that way, she wondered how Paul must be feeling, after giving so much of himself at every performance.

It was the end of September when they arrived in Cannes. Still summer in the south of France, and Angela felt a thrill of excitement as they drove into the city. Its huge white buildings and wide expensive streets were all she'd imagined them to be. She glanced at the street map in her hand.

"Do you know the hotel where we're staying, Paul?"

He shook his head. "It shouldn't be difficult to find," he said briefly. "Near the *plage,* the beach, and one of the newest and biggest Cannes has to offer, according to Charlie."

As they turned onto the coast road, the brilliant blue of the Mediterranean came into view, dotted with hundreds of boats of every description, from sleek white cruisers to ocean-going liners. The whole bay jostled with masts and golden-skinned young men and girls. It was a picture-book scene, and the blue water looked deliciously inviting.

"Oh, it's beautiful," she breathed. "I didn't think to bring a swimsuit. I'll have to buy one right away! I can't wait to get into that water!"

"Don't you have a bikini with you? It's about all the girls wear around here," he said mockingly.

She glared at him. It was just the taunt she'd have expected from him. As he stopped the car outside the hotel he gave her his sardonic smile.

"Maybe you're afraid of going to the beach with

me," he suggested coolly. "And don't think you can get away with not bringing a swimsuit. The shops are full of them. When we've unpacked you can buy what you need. Let's see how keen you are to have a swim, or are you going to come all the way to the south of France and then chicken out?"

Why did he have to keep putting her on the defensive? Did he really think she couldn't cope with lying on a beach with him for half an hour? She pushed down the little shiver of excitement at the thought. Anyway, there'd be dozens of other people there. He wouldn't be able to try anything on a crowded beach!

"All right, you're on," she said flatly. "Maybe I've got a sneaking desire to see that supposedly perfect physique of yours too. I might even discover a few flaws!"

She forced a smile now, and Paul's eyes flinched a little. He just couldn't take it, Angela thought exultantly. As long as he was the one doing all the teasing, it was all right, but he didn't like to be thought of as less than perfect.

They checked into the hotel. Their rooms were on the same floor, but not adjoining, Angela saw to her relief. They were overlooking the sea, and each room had a little balcony outside with white wrought-iron railings and sun canopies, with beach furniture to add to the illusion that they were here on holiday. She wasn't, she reminded herself, and when she'd found the number of the Cannes theater where Paul was to perform, she rang through at once to check on the rehearsal arrangements.

"Such efficiency!" his voice said mockingly behind her as she finished. She whirled, not having heard him come in. He'd already changed into light slacks and a red checked shirt, open nearly to the waist. Around his neck he wore a silver medallion she'd seen several times before. On his bronze chest the dark hair curled against his skin.

137

"Isn't that what you wanted?" she said jerkily. "An efficient P.R.O.?"

He was suddenly across the room and pulling her into his arms.

"You know quite well what I want," he spoke right against her mouth. She thought he was going to kiss her, but instead he pushed her away none too gently. "And I'll have it before we're through, my sweet angel. Though it would be all the sweeter if you wanted it too. A one-sided affair has never appealed to me."

"You mean you can't bear to think every woman isn't panting after you!" she whipped back at him.

"Something like that!"

His chauvinism made her squirm. Why the dickens couldn't she have fallen in love with someone like Tim, with his easy, uncomplicated character? Why did it have to be Paul Blake, of all people? She turned away, before her feelings were reflected in her eyes. For all his arrogance, she still wanted to be in his arms, and each time he held her there she had to fight against her own instincts. But she wouldn't give in. She wouldn't end up as one more scalp on his belt.

"It's morning rehearsals here," she said evenly. "They'll be using the theater in the afternoons for private functions. I hope you have no objections?"

"None at all. We can relax in the afternoons, once the day's business is attended to. I shall feel fully relaxed by the evenings if we take advantage of this glorious Mediterranean beach."

"We'll need towels," she speculated.

"They provide colored beach towels on request, I'm told. And there's a beach shop in the foyer, so we don't even need to go searching for your bikini. We can get it right here."

"*I* can get it," Angela retorted. She picked up her bag. "I don't need your help, thank you."

She waited for him to leave her room, but he sprawled out on the bed with a grin.

138

"I'll wait here. I can't believe it! What will you come back with, I wonder? A Victorian striped garment with elasticized ankles? Though you'd look good even in that——"

Angela swept out of the room while he was still talking. She wasn't going to pander to his taunts anyway. She would have bought a one-piece suit, but they didn't cater to such conservative tastes in the hotel shop. The only swimsuits were the briefest bikinis Angela had ever seen. She looked at them dubiously, and then thought recklessly, so what? If he thought she was going to turn up in the most modest suit she could find, he was going to get a shock.

Fifteen minutes later Angela was back in the hotel bedroom with the bikini and a beach bag to hold towels, suntan lotion and sunglasses. She felt a surge of excitement. She was in the south of France, and for that afternoon at least, she was going to relax and just be a tourist.

There was a note from Paul on her bed.

"Knock on my door when you're ready. Hope I'm in for a surprise!"

Her mouth twisted. She slipped out of her shirt and slacks and into the silky coolness of the sky-blue bikini. There were little ties at the sides of the wispy pants, and a halter neck on the top, with matching ties at the back. There was very little of it, and Angela balked a little as she saw her reflection in the mirror.

Her smooth satiny waist dipped in deliciously between the soft curving hips and the firmness of her breasts. It left very little to the imagination. Turning a little to see the rear effect, at least she knew she was trim from all angles. The shape of her spine was just visible enough for her to be well covered with firm flesh without being bony. And flesh was the word, Angela thought uneasily. But she'd bought the thing now, and it was too late to have second thoughts about wearing it.

She slipped a thin sundress over the bikini and stuffed some pants into her beach bag. Whether the bikini was intended for swimming or not, nothing was going to keep her out of that enticing blue water once she'd done a bit of sunbathing.

Paul had obviously requested towels, because there were two large striped beach towels on her bed. She added them to the contents of her beach bag, drew a deep breath and went to knock on Paul's door.

"I'm disappointed," he grinned as he saw her. "I'd expected a private viewing."

"You'll just have to be patient then, won't you?" She spoke lightly, but her heart was beating so fast it felt as if it was jumping in her chest. They had already had some fairly intimate moments, and Paul had made no secret of his desire for her; but this was something different. Lying half naked on a Mediterranean beach in the hot sun had every promise of being a very pleasurable, if not highly sensual experience, and they both knew it.

The beach was only yards away from the hotel. Even the pavement was hot beneath Angela's rope sandals, and when they had walked down the short stone steps to the beach, she felt the sand slide over her toes. It was luxuriously hot too. The sun was blazing, and the beach well populated. Everywhere she looked, golden-skinned girls and bronzed young men basked in the sultry heat of the Mediterranean sun. Beyond the expanse of glorious, fine sand, the blue water was like diamond-studded silk.

"I think this will do for us," Paul said easily, as they found a patch of sand to call their own beneath a craggy outcrop of rocks. He grinned at her as he stretched out nonchalantly on the sand, his eyes faintly mocking. "Well then, my lovely. It's the moment of truth. Or are you going to tell me now that you chickened out of buying a bikini after all?"

Angela tightened her lips. Why did he always have to

make her feel so acutely on the defensive with him? And so ridiculously naive, when she wasn't really like that at all! She spread out her towel without answering or looking at him. Silently she slid out of the sundress covering her bikini, and heard Paul's soft, low intake of breath. She couldn't resist glancing at him. She wouldn't have been human if she hadn't wanted his reaction to be favorable, and she wasn't disappointed. His dark eyes widened as he took his time in letting his gaze wander over every little bit of her, as if he wanted to impress her shape in his mind forever.

"I wish you wouldn't look at me that way," she said nervously.

"Why not? You've nothing to be ashamed of, Angela. On the contrary. I imagine there are plenty of girls who'd envy a figure like yours." His voice was frankly admiring, but he could still manage to make the color run up her cheeks at the way his eyes lingered on her. She sat down quickly on the large towel, intending to lie back and close her eyes and soak up the sun. She had to do two jobs at once, she thought, acquire a tan, and escape the disturbing intensity of Paul's gaze.

She fumbled in the beach bag for the suntan lotion. It slipped out of her fingers onto the sand, and Paul picked it up.

"You aren't going to deny me one of life's pleasures, are you?" He held the bottle away from her teasingly, spinning open the lid and pouring the golden liquid into his palm. Before she could protest, he was circling it gently into her shoulders, her arms and her throat, to where the creamy flesh swelled out of the brief bikini top.

"Don't, please." Her voice was low and strained.

His hand left her at once, but it only moved lower, to caress her midriff with the fragrant lotion. It was driving her quickly crazy! She gave a small sigh and lay back on the towel while his sensitive hands moved slowly up and down her legs with the suntan lotion.

141

Whoever invented the stuff knew what it was all about, she thought dizzily.

"I'll do your back later," he said softly. "Now you can do the same for me."

Her eyes flew open. *Oh no*, she thought, *I couldn't!* Paul's eyes mocked her as he stripped off the red shirt and slacks. He leaned on one elbow as he lay full-length on his own towel. His swimming briefs were white, laced at the sides, and started well below his waist. Angela shifted her gaze fast. He had a magnificent torso, she had to admit, with wide shoulders tapering to a neat waist and narrow hips. The light covering of dark hair on his body accentuated the impression of virility. He lay on his back on his towel and handed her the suntan lotion calmly.

Angela took it wordlessly. Paul closed his eyes. She tipped a circle of lotion on his chest and heard him catch his breath at its coldness. She poured some more.

"Unless you want me to slide right through the beach, you'd better do something with that, hadn't you?" his voice came lazily.

Gingerly at first, Angela began massaging the lotion into his firm, taut chest. His skin was already tanned to a deep bronze, and the short dark hairs glistened where the lotion touched them. She did his chest and waist and then his arms. He pointed to his legs as she stopped, his eyes still closed, but with a half-smile on his lips. He was enjoying this, she fumed, but she was enjoying it too. She was enjoying it far too much, she admitted. She sat back on her heels when she'd finished, but her fingers tingled, and she could still feel the texture of his skin beneath them even when she no longer touched it.

"Turn over," she ordered. She didn't want to see his fine figure spread out in front of her like an offering to the gods. He opened his eyes and looked at her for a long moment, and then he did as she told him. Angela gasped. Running diagonally across the lower part of his back and disappearing into his swimming trunks were several long scars, which could only be the result of continued beatings.

"My God," she whispered involuntarily. His face was turned sideways, away from her.

"Go on," he said brutally. "You wanted to see my flaws, and now you've seen them. They won't bite, but I'd prefer it if you didn't rub too hard with the suntan stuff on them."

Angela bit back the habitual retort. There was a note of bruised pride in Paul's voice, that his perfect body was marred in this way. She wanted to cry out that it didn't matter, that it would make no difference to her, but she knew instinctively it wouldn't be the reaction he wanted. She used the lotion steadily, just as he asked, skimming the ugly scars with the lightest of touches.

"Who did it to you?" she mumbled finally, because she found it impossible to ignore it any longer. Paul twisted to look at her. There was pain in his eyes, but she realized it was the pain of remembering as he spoke. His voice was curt.

"My father. He called it the incentive to produce perfection. He desperately wanted me to be the best pianist in the world, and when I didn't come up to his standards he beat me. I prefer to keep covered up, but short of sunbathing in a track suit, I have no choice if I want to enjoy the delights of the Riviera."

Angela wanted to say the scars weren't that bad. They were certainly not off-putting to a woman, but she had the feeling he'd only think she was patronizing him. She yearned to say something comforting, but she was tongue-tied. She began to understand him better, though. He had achieved perfection in his chosen profession, but she believed he would have done that despite his taskmaster of a father and his unloving mother. Paul's own personality demanded perfection from himself and from others. It was a hard image to live up to.

But she hardly knew how to answer him, and chose instead to say nothing. She lay face-down on her towel, not wanting him to see how his revelation had affected her.

"No one's taking any notice of anyone else around here," she mumbled at last. "I don't think you need worry——"

"Just what I've been telling you, my sweet. So lie still and I'll put some of this suntan stuff on your back—unless you want to end up looking like a lobster."

She felt the coolness of the lotion in the small of her back before she could decide whether to protest or not. Then her eyes closed as his hands moved against her skin. They weren't too gentle at first, as if he was still caught up in the old story he'd told her. But gradually his touch grew more caressing, kneading her flesh softly and sensuously, out over her shoulders and behind the tiny straps of her bikini top, curving into the dip of her waist and flaring out to her hips. His touch was pure magic, dulling her senses with its rhythmic movements to give her a lethargic floating sensation.

Then his hands moved lower, over the length of her legs with the smooth satiny lotion, making her skin feel warm and pampered. But now she was no longer lethargic. His manipulations tightened her throat and sent the blood pulsing through her veins in exciting awareness. Still she kept her face averted, her eyes firmly closed.

Chapter Nine

They stayed at the beach for an hour. As soon as the hot sun began to prickle on her skin, Angela knew it was time to stop basking on the beach.

"I'm going to have a swim," she told Paul. His skin was deepening rapidly with the sun on it, making the scars far less noticeable. He murmured something, but she didn't wait to hear what it was. That blue water was too inviting.

Stepping into the warm soft saltiness of it was like heaven. She waded out, letting the little waves caress her body like gentle hands. The water was the softest she had ever known, and it was an incredible feeling.

The next minute she realized that Paul was beside her, as his hand reached out for hers. She let it remain in his grasp as they waded out together until there was no more sand beneath their feet, and Angela turned over onto her back, floating in the deliciously buoyant water. Paul did the same, their fingers still touching.

An energetic swimmer raced past them, splashing their faces, and the sudden movement made Angela automatically tread water. Instantly Paul's arms were round her, his mouth salty on hers as he took advantage of her change of position to kiss her. She fought him off laughingly for a moment, though just a little panicky at finding herself out of her depth, but then the laughter died in her throat as his kisses became more brutal and demanding.

His strong legs locked around hers and held her fast. He was embracing her with every inch of his body, and she could feel every sinewy part of him pressing tightly against her, with only a sparse thin layer of material separating them. It was the most erotic sensation she had ever known.

Their bodies molded so perfectly together, as if they were made for each other. Angela could no more resist letting her arms wind around his neck and caressing the wet hair at the nape of his neck than deny that the sun shone high above them like a golden god. His salty kisses were intoxicating her. . . .

Suddenly she heard Paul give a strangled oath and he twisted away from her clinging embrace, swimming away from her with powerful strokes. Angela trod water numbly, watching him streak away from her. Trickles of water ran down her face, and she couldn't have said at that moment whether they were droplets of the ocean or her own salty tears.

Slowly she turned back toward the shoreline, paddling gently with her hands through the crystal-clear water, and trying in vain to understand the complexity of the man. He was nowhere in sight as she walked slowly back to their patch of sand, and by the time he did return, she had dried herself and wore the sundress to keep the burning rays of the sun off her salt-sprayed shoulders.

Paul picked up his towel and began rubbing at his legs to brush the sand from them. He pulled his shirt around himself and tugged on his trousers.

"I think it's time we went back to the hotel." His voice was clipped. "I daresay you'll want a shower before dinner."

Angela felt her throat constrict. Such a little while ago she'd been held in his arms in a magical embrace that had been more sensual than anything she had ever experienced. Had it meant so little to him? She couldn't believe it. She looked at him, her mouth trembling a little. Her hair curled damply round her head like a cherub's, and she couldn't understand why he didn't seem to want to look at her.

"Paul—what have I done?" she heard herself say haltingly. She didn't want to appear bewildered, but that was how he made her feel—like a naughty child who'd done something to displease the teacher, but wasn't too sure what it was.

"Nothing," he told her. "Except be yourself."

It didn't make sense to her. She wondered if he could even explain it to himself. When they had collected all their belongings, they walked back to the hotel in silence, their progress stopped only by a beautiful, olive-skinned girl in a red bikini, who asked Paul for his autograph.

"It is M. Paul Blake, no?" She had a soft, throaty voice, and Angela watched in amazement as the instant charm was switched on. Paul was the complete professional again, his eyes smiling appreciatively at the girl's rounded shape, all his aggressiveness gone. He scrawled his name on the old envelope the girl held out to him, and she looked up adoringly into his eyes.

"I will be in a front-row seat at your first concert here, M. Blake," the girl went on huskily. "Would you please sign the envelope for Marie-Hélène? That is my name," she added for his benefit.

"Then I'll be sure to dedicate one of the pieces especially to you," he said softly. "To Marie-Hélène," he repeated the name she told him.

As long as it wasn't "Autumn Leaves," thought Angela jealously. That belonged to *her*. She gave a sigh of relief. At least the girl had lightened Paul's mood again, even if the little encounter had sharpened her own. It was ridiculous to feel jealous. There were many girls who would give their eye teeth to have Paul Blake smile into their eyes and dedicate a piece of music to them. So why should one more make any difference?

It was just that they had always seemed so anonymous before. They hadn't had beauty and a personality that had quickened the interest in Paul's eyes. Angela knew she was being completely dog-in-the-manger about him. She wouldn't give in to him, but she had no desire to see his interest stray elsewhere, as it surely would, eventually. But then, it was going to anyway, when this mockery of an engagement ended. But by then, Angela had no intention of being around. She couldn't bear to watch while he charmed somebody else.

"I'll take that shower," she said briefly at her bedroom door. "I have a few things to sort through before dinner, so shall I see you in the dining room?"

"As you wish."

Angela went into her own room. It was warm, and she opened the windows wide, letting a soft breeze blow in from the balcony. In the shower she let the lukewarm water trickle over her bare shoulders and her newly tanned body. She tanned easily and quickly, and there was only a small part of her body now that wasn't a deep honey color. She patted herself dry with a soft towel and slipped her arms into a silky robe. It was too hot to dress yet. Even for the Riviera, it was an exceptionally hot summer, and the air was almost stifling without the sea breeze.

There was a knock on her door. She opened it to find Paul standing outside. There was no trace of a smile on his face, and once again she had the feeling of being the naughty schoolgirl facing the stern headmaster. The feeling unnerved her, and with a jerky movement she tightened the loose belt of her robe as if to give her confidence. Naturally he noticed it.

"I'm going for a walk," he said curtly. "If you'll let me have the beach towels, I'll drop them in the hotel laundry on my way out."

He stepped inside the room after her. Angela rummaged inside the beach bag, suddenly nervous. She could see that Paul had showered too. His dark hair was damp against his well-shaped head, and the tang of aftershave and body lotion clung to his skin. As always, he made her acutely aware of herself, and the fact that she was only wearing the silky robe.

She told herself irritably that it was completely illogical to feel so vulnerable, when for most of the afternoon she'd worn only two scraps of material on the beach, and his eyes had feasted on her. It made no difference. Though she was covered with a robe, there was a smoldering look in his eyes that she recognized.

She realized the belt of her robe was only tied in a single knot. Pulling it as tightly as she had done had only given it leeway for slipping against the movements of her body, and the shiny material wasn't holding together as she pulled out the towels from the beach bag and handed them to him silently. He took them from her and tossed them to the floor. Angela's heart began to pound as he moved slowly toward her.

"I thought you said something about taking a walk," she said as evenly as she could. She still hadn't forgotten his abruptness at the beach. Did he think he could turn her emotions on and off at will? She wasn't equipped for dealing with a situation like this, she realized weakly. At least she had always known where she was with Tim.

Paul's hands rested on her shoulders. Through the silky robe they felt as hot as fire. She could feel the tension in him. His thumbs made small sensual circles on the tops of her arms, and she gave a shiver that was pure involuntary reaction to his touch. The movements stopped at once.

"Do I offend you so much?" he said slowly. She shook her head mutely, loosening the damp tendrils of her hair. He didn't offend her at all, but she had already learned how dangerous it could be to lower her guard when he was around.

"I thought it was I who had offended you in some way at the beach." Her voice was unsteady, and she

149

heard him give a small groan as he took her in his arms.
His heart beat rapidly against hers.

"How can I expect you to understand my reasons,
sweet Angela? If I say I'm so used to taking everything
I want, you'll think I'm an arrogant swine. And you,
with the looks of an angel, are so aptly named, yet
there's some little devil inside you that can drive a man
wild. I don't think you realize how devilish you can be,
with your look of innocence that can change in an
instant to the wantonness of a very desirable woman."
His voice had deepened as he spoke, and Angela ran
her tongue over her dry lips.

"It's in no way intentional," she said faintly. And if
she had this ability to drive him wild, just what did he
think he was doing to her? She was trembling inside at
the nearness of him now. The way his hands were
traveling slowly downward, over the length of her arms
and back again, sent shivers running through her like
shooting flames.

"Intentional or not, you're everything I desire in a
woman," Paul whispered huskily against her cheek. His
skin was still slightly damp from his shower, the scent of
soap and lotion tantalizing her still more as his cheek
brushed her own. If she were to move her head even a
fraction, his mouth would be on hers and she knew it. It
would have taken a superhuman effort for her to resist
such a movement. And she was all too human where
Paul was concerned.

Seconds later her body seemed to have a will of its
own as it molded itself to Paul's, and his lips claimed
hers in a feather-light kiss. As their lips clung together,
the kiss deepened into one of hungry longing. Angie's
senses swam as the embrace went on and on, as if
neither of them could bear to break away. For those
sweet moments, Paul belonged to her utterly, and she
felt dizzy with the joy of it.

They were standing very close to Angela's bed. She
hardly knew how they came to be sitting on it, still

locked in that enchanted embrace. She was warmed by Paul's arms, thrilled by the sheer animal magnetism of him, stirred beyond measure by the knowledge that he wanted her. He could have any woman in the world, but it was her that he wanted.

"My own lovely girl," he breathed against her lips, the soft movement sending new shafts of desire through every part of her. She felt his hands gentle on her shoulders again, and she seemed unable to resist as he moved her very slowly backward on to the pillow. She hardly registered lifting her feet from the carpet to lie on the bed. Her breathing was very shallow as Paul lay down beside her, easing the long hard length of his body onto the coverlet until it partially covered hers.

She could hear his ragged breathing close to her cheek. Nothing seemed quite real any more, nothing but the desire that was holding them captive.

The silky robe was being pushed aside by his seeking hands, and she felt his sensitive fingers on her skin, stroking and caressing. She could hardly breathe for the shock of what was happening, and the pulsating reactions she couldn't deny.

She should protest! She should lash out at him with her fists, bite his shoulder through the thin shirt he wore, laugh in his face in a way that would infuriate him and accuse him of being no more than an animal.

Paul's mouth was covering hers in a kiss that parted her lips before she could formulate any coherent words, and she felt the wild sweet abandonment touching her soul.

But even as she shivered with the thrill of his caresses, some semblance of sanity made her twist her head away from him before she lost all control. If she let this happen, it would be his triumph, proof that he could break down all her resistance through his charisma alone. There was still no mention of loving her.

"Don't do this, Paul." The words were almost torn out of her in a thick whisper. She was helpless if he persisted. She prayed he didn't guess how far she was tempted.

"Why not?" He was aggressively male as his lips moved downward, softly kissing her throat and her shoulders, moving ecstatically down to meet her honeyed breasts. Angela caught her breath at their tingling response.

"Why not, my angel?" he murmured softly against them. "When you want it as much as I do? This was inevitable, and you know it. We both knew it from the moment we saw each other. Admit it now. Admit that you want me, Angela. *Don't* you?"

"Paul . . ." she breathed his name in a little sigh.

"Say you want me, Angela." His voice was urgent now.

Affirmation trembled on her lips. Yes, yes, yes, she wanted him. The words shrieked inside her. She wanted him, needed him, loved him, totally and forever. But the words were never said. The telephone at the side of her bed jarred into her bemused mind, making her gasp them back.

"Let it ring," Paul said harshly. "It won't be anything important."

It went on ringing like an intrusion into their privacy, and Angela knew she couldn't just ignore it. The businesswoman in her struggled to the fore. It might be the theater, or the hotel manager with some query. She wrenched herself out of Paul's arms and swung her legs off the bed, dragging the silky robe around her with shaking hands to cover her nakedness, her face burning as she grabbed the receiver.

"Yes?" The word was a croak. Her throat was so dry she could hardly speak.

She heard Paul's furious expletive as he moved away from the bed and strode toward the door. She waved wildly at him as she heard the receptionist's words. He paused, but frustrated anger was stamped all over him.

"I'm sorry to disturb you, Mademoiselle," the voice said in rapid French. "But I cannot locate Blake, and Comte Vincennes is in the foyer. Can you help?"

Angela couldn't honestly have said whether she felt a wild rush of relief that Jacques had arrived at that moment, or the sharp sting of disappointment. Paul tormented her so much she hardly understood her own feelings any more.

"M. Blake will be down immediately," she said to the girl. "Thank you for the message."

She put the receiver down, her hands held tightly together to stop them shaking. She swallowed hard, hoping Paul couldn't guess how near she'd been to being whatever he desired of her. He looked at her, his face as hard as marble. It was almost incredible to believe that only minutes ago he'd been an ardent lover.

"Jacques is here," she told him jerkily.

"So I heard."

Suddenly there seemed nothing more to say. The distance between them was so vast it might have been an ocean. Paul's male pride was badly wounded, and he looked at her as if he hated her. Angela flinched visibly, wishing with all her heart she hadn't hurt him so, and cursing the romantic idiot that she was. All this trauma because of one word she wanted to hear from his lips.

He saw her flinch, but to Paul's eyes it was a convulsive little shudder. It shamed him with a suddenness that took him by surprise. He wasn't used to feeling shame, but as she stood there, so defensive and childlike, clutching the silky robe around her like some ravished maiden of old, he felt a basic urge to take her and fold her in his arms and tell her that no one was ever going to hurt her while he was around, as though he were a knight in shining armor.

His own feelings were becoming inexplicable to him, and with a last muttered oath he told her shortly to get dressed and meet them downstairs in the coffee lounge in half an hour.

After he'd gone, Angela wilted on the bed. All her life she'd believed in the kind of love that meant a one-man, one-woman commitment. She'd always kept well away from men who played the field. There was always something slightly pathetic about the middle-aged womanizers she'd come in contact with in her career, who were never able to resist flirting with every available woman, to preen themselves when they got any response, no matter how trivial.

She'd always vowed she'd never fall for such a man. And she'd been warned from the start. Charlie Cass had warned her of Paul's roving eye. She'd seen the photo of Claudette Dubois in Paul's London home and seen the lady herself reveal her claws. She'd seen how he basked in the adulation of the stage-door girls, and that very day, Marie-Hélène had gone away with stars in her eyes. Why, of all men on earth, did she have to fall in love with Paul Blake?

The answer soared into her mind. Because he was everything she ever wanted. She loved his looks, the way he walked, his animal aggressiveness, his sudden tenderness. She adored the way he drew magic from his fingertips when he performed at the piano. She loved to watch those long, elegant fingers of his stroke the keys with as much sensitivity as he'd stroked her body.

Angela jerked her thoughts back from such treacherous sweet memories. She didn't want to remember those moments when she'd almost been totally his, though she doubted if she would ever forget them. They were imprinted forever on her soul.

She forced herself to remember that Paul and Jacques would be waiting for her in the coffee lounge downstairs. At least with Jacques around, there would be no more assaults on her emotions, though of course there would be the pretense of the engagement to keep up. When she had dressed in a fresh white shirt and blue linen skirt, Angela slid the Victorian ring on her finger, staring at its beautiful emerald circlet with a catch at her throat. It was an antique ring, made to be worn in love. How many other wearers had gazed at it with joy in their hearts, knowing it was the symbol of being loved? She turned away abruptly to make up her face in the dressing-table mirror as deftly as she could, and ignore the shadowed look in her hazel eyes.

Jacques appeared to notice nothing unusual about her. He rose to greet her as soon as she went into the coffee lounge, kissing both cheeks and holding her at arm's length to admire her new suntan.

"You look even more radiant than when I saw you in Paris, *chérie*," he said. "The south of France must be suiting you very well—or could it be the effects of love that give you such a lovely glow? I envy my old friend his good fortune."

Angela didn't dare to look at Paul. She smiled brightly at Jacques.

"It's good to see you again, Jacques. Will you be able to stay for the concerts?"

He nodded. "Oh yes, I intend to remain with you now until the end of the tour. That is, if you have no objections? It's partly professional, to get some more copy and photos for the magazine, and partly pleasure, because I love this part of the country. And also to have a little more of your company, dear Angela. I don't see why Paul should have you all to himself. There'll be time enough for that when you're married."

He glanced from one to the other, sensing a sudden silence about them. No doubt a lovers' tiff, Jacques speculated. Such things happened, and the loving would be all the sweeter when it was resolved. Knowing Paul, he was sure he wouldn't be able to keep at arm's length from his lovely Angela for very long.

"Have you ordered coffee?" Angela said hurriedly.

"We waited for you," Paul told her. "And we don't mind having Jacques along as chaperone, do we, darling? Perhaps it's just as well, then I can save some of my energies for the concert platform, instead of using it in other ways."

He was mocking her, but Jacques obviously took his words in the way Paul had intended, and laughed indulgently. He naturally assumed that they were lovers in every sense of the word, Angela thought furiously. Paul had no right to speak so suggestively. But her eyes betrayed none of the fury she felt. Instead she smiled sweetly into Paul's eyes and told him not to use all of it up at the theater. They were sparring with each other, but Jacques was completely unaware of it.

But after all, it was a relief to have him around. As Angela had surmised, he was a buffer between her and Paul, and his easy manner kept the tensions from rising too high between them, though both of them were well aware that they still simmered below the surface.

Jacques flirted outrageously with her, sure in his own mind that the engaged pair would know he was only teasing. Neither of them chose to disillusion him about the real relationship between them, and in defiance to Paul's sometimes touchy remarks about her playing up to Jacques more than was necessary, she responded even more. It didn't mean a thing, and she knew it. But it soothed her bruised feelings to know that Jacques sincerely admired her, and thought Paul extremely fortunate. He told her so yet again after the last performance in Cannes, while they waited for Paul to sign the inevitable autographs. They sat in the theater's small bar with a carafe of wine, and Angela sipped the red liquid, feeling its fire warm her. Her smile twisted a little.

"I'm not so sure Paul would agree with you," she murmured, and then bit her lip as Jacques looked at her in astonishment. Now there was a stupid thing to say when she and Paul were supposed to be head over heels in love! She amended it hurriedly.

"What I mean is, he's known so many lovely women before me, Jacques! Women like Claudette Dubois——"

Jacques' hand closed over hers.

"But you're the one he chose, *chérie*. Those others—" he gave a typical French shrug of dismissal—"they meant nothing in his life. They were butterflies, no more. Pretty little things to give a moment's pleasure."

Angela couldn't imagine the statuesque Claudette being likened to a butterfly. Nor was she wholly comfortable about Jacques' remarks. The "others" sounded like an army of women, all slipping through Paul's demanding fingers for a moment's pleasure. Her instincts told her that he wasn't as shallow as the words suggested, but there *had* been women. And Claudette had been one of them.

Jacques's fingers tipped up her chin as her spirits momentarily drooped. He smiled gently into her eyes.

"Cheer up, *chérie*. You and Paul are like two sides of the same coin. What you have is untouchable by others."

It was a lovely sentiment, but Paul chose that moment to appear with some of the fans buzzing around him. His smile became fixed as he saw his fiancée and his friend, apparently in a very intimate little moment, with Jacques's finger beneath her chin, gazing adoringly into her eyes. It looked for all the world as if he were about to kiss her.

Angela flushed with annoyance as she saw that one of the girls hanging round Paul was the girl from the beach, Marie-Hélène, looking chic and beautiful in a white silk dress split well up her thigh, her mouth dewy and soft as she gazed into Paul's face. She'd had her piece of music, Angela thought cattily. And it had been "Clair de Lune" too, dedicated on the first night.

"Look who couldn't resist coming to the theater again." Paul drew her toward them. "That's what I call dedication!"

Marie-Hélène laughed throatily. "I only came because of you, *chéri*. You 'ave such beautiful 'ands. I could not resist seeing them again."

Paul was enjoying this. "And I thought it was just for the music." He grinned knowingly.

To Angela's fury he invited her to have supper with them, but she refused sorrowfully as she had a previous engagement.

"What a shame. My friend the comte is so taken up with my fiancée I thought a fourth companion might have evened things up a bit." The smile was still on Paul's face, but his words were barbed enough for Angela to know he was displeased. The nerve of him! She knew he was elated as always that the concerts had been a success, and that he'd need to unwind. He needed smiling faces around him, and no hint of dissonance. She knew that, and usually she reacted as he wanted and smoothed the way for him; but tonight was the exception. As they rose to join Paul in the manager's office for the farewell formalities, and Marie-Hélène went off into the night, Angela tucked her arm in Jacques's and gave his a little squeeze.

"Yes, what a shame. Jacques and I were just beginning to get to know each other properly," she said in a brittle voice.

"Hey, come on, you'll be making him jealous in a minute," Jacques said easily, not really believing it.

"Oh, I doubt it." She smiled into Paul's eyes. "It's just a little *game* we play, isn't it, darling?"

Chapter Ten

Jacques's presence was obviously a relief to both of them, Angela thought. Though they drove separately to Marseille, she and Paul arrived at the hotel in a wide tree-lined boulevard almost at the same time as Jacques. She was happy to let the two men go off together while she attended to the business of the tour. She was completely on top of all that was required of her—ironically so, since it would probably be the last time she had to deal with any of Paul's affairs.

The prospect of returning to England and finding another flat and another job was a bleak one. Neither task would be all that difficult with her qualifications, but the thought of not being with Paul was devastating. It was better not to let her mind dwell on such things.

Besides, before all that happened, there were the five days in Marseille, culminating in the three nightly performances, and then the week at the Château Vincennes, in the Camargue. She'd be looking forward to that enormously, if it weren't for Claudette.

The five days passed quickly. In public, Paul was his usual charming self, and attentive to his new fiancée. The usual newshounds got their stories and clicked their cameras, and Jacques got his own special story of how a concert tour was undertaken, with personal interviews with the artist and his assistant. His magazine had never had such privileged information, he told them with a chuckle.

* * *

Angela felt ridiculously emotional as she realized that Paul was about to play his last piece in his last concert of the tour. The audience was as receptive as ever, and she watched Paul give his quick smile of appreciation. For a moment he turned and looked directly at her in the wings, and she felt her heartbeat quicken. She hoped he wouldn't make any embarrassing reference this time about his lady with hair the color of autumn leaves. She knew without being told that he could change his mind about his comments with no prior thought.

He spoke into the microphone on the piano.

"Ladies and gentlemen, I give you my final piece, 'Autumn Leaves.'" He paused for a calculated second. "To Angela."

She felt choked. It was the first time in the whole tour he'd mentioned her name. Always it had been the veiled reference to the lady the audience surmised was somebody special in his life. She heard the faintest rustle of interest among them, and knew it would be reported in the newspapers tomorrow. It would be a romantic and significant note on which to end the reports of the successful tour. Even Jacques would make the most of this.

They'd have to tell Jacques the truth, she thought. Why should he be a party to the deception? And then Claudette would know, and the other guests at the château, and it might be an embarrassing situation. It would be assumed that one or other of them was suffering with a broken heart. Suddenly, she changed her mind.

Try as she might, it was impossible not to let the music affect her. It would always be especially poignant to her now, even though he gave it the strictly highbrow interpretation that lifted it far from the realms of contemporary music. She tried to think dispassionately as she stood in the wings of the theater, wondering if all music could be treated this way—the classical jazzed up, the more popular pieces raised to symphonic importance by the sensitive touch of a born musician.

She tried not to listen to the melody that was slowly but insidiously filtering through the minor chords as Paul played on, cleverly relaxing the classical hold on the music, and bringing it to its more usual rendition for his appreciative audience. He gave them everything, Angela thought, with a catch in her throat. She wouldn't let herself register the fact that he'd as good as told the world now that he played it just for her.

He should never have mentioned her by name, she thought, the salty tears stinging her eyes as the music washed over her in a rising crescendo. He had no right to do this to her, when they both knew this farce of an engagement would soon end. It should never have begun. Angela bit her lip. The magic between them, if that's what it was, had begun from the moment they met, just as Paul had said.

The sound of thunderous applause made her realize the music had ended, and Paul was standing to a great ovation. The Marseille crowd loved him. They shouted his name. She felt her heart leap as she realized they called for her too. *Oh no,* she cringed. She wasn't used to this. Paul turned to her, holding out his hand and drawing her onto the stage, his voice whispering in her ear.

"It's all right, darling, you'll be with me," he said softly. "They want you—listen to them! They want to see this lovely lady with hair the color of autumn leaves. Don't disappoint them—please!"

He was high on the adoration of his fans. She was his crowning moment. As if she walked in a dream, Angela let herself be led out onto the stage. Her legs shook so much she felt she'd never get there, but Paul's arm was around her, his fingers firm on her shoulder. She shared in the applause, and she knew a little of how it felt to be the center of attention. She couldn't blame him for wanting more of it, for needing it so much, after the pressure from his mother and the wrath of his father, and the perfection he sought so determinedly.

She smiled up into his face, as exalted by the moment as Paul, and there was a sudden cheer of approval as he bent his head and kissed her in front of the audience. She hadn't anticipated the kiss, but it only lasted a moment and then Paul held up his hand for quiet.

"Isn't she lovely?" he asked expansively, and a little roar of agreement met his words. Angela could have danced with pleasure. She was enveloped by a warm and heady feeling.

"This is my Angela, ladies and gentlemen, the lady who's going to be my wife, and very soon, I hope."

Angela's gasp was lost in the renewed applause. He should never have made it so public, she thought furiously. The engagement could have died a simple death if no more mention had been made of it. Now every newspaper interested in Paul's concert was going to make the most of this. Even from the audience flash bulbs were popping as he hugged her close to him and told her to smile.

By the time the audience finally let them go and the curtain came down, Jacques was across the stage to put his arms round them both, a look of delight on his face.

"That was a master stroke, Paul. I've got to hand it to you. You know how to draw an audience." His words were teasing, but he obviously believed Angela had been in on this, and saw nothing wrong in his comment.

"Oh, he knows all right," she spluttered. "Anything for a bit of extra publicity."

"Darling, they loved you!" Paul pulled her into his arms as if to reassure her, and grinned at Jacques. "I should have realized Angela's not used to standing out there. It's pretty traumatic."

He held her tightly, and she knew he was mutely asking her not to make a scene. Especially as the manager of the theater was approaching them with outstretched arms at the success of the concert and to express his own congratulations and to ask them and the comte to join him and the staff for cocktails in his office. Jacques gave the couple a puzzled look for a moment, and then Angela lifted her flushed face and nodded slightly at Paul. She'd agreed to his outrageous suggestion about the engagement, and she'd play it out to the bitter end. She knew how to go by the rules, even if he didn't.

"I'm all right now, Paul," she said unsteadily. "As you said—it was a bit overwhelming."

She felt his sigh of relief. His lips brushed her cheek.

"Thank you, Angie." The simple whispered words in her ear took her by surprise by their apparent sincerity.

She went with him to the manager's office in a state of bewilderment. If she lived to be a hundred, she'd never fully understand the complexity of the man. One minute he was arrogant and brutal in his wants; the next, he could be so tender as to take her breath away.

But at last all the formalities were over and the tour was officially ended. As if summer had ended too, the sun had deserted them temporarily the next morning when they started out on the road for Arles and the Château Vincennes.

They struck off from the Arles road a few miles south of the town. Eventually Angela saw they were approaching what looked like a large wooded area, behind which, Paul told her shortly, was the château.

He pointed to where a group of the Camargue horses were being rounded up by several young men. They looked more like Spanish *vaqueros* than Wild West cowboys, but it was the horses that caught Angela's attention. They were exactly as she had imagined, pure white with long flowing manes and tails, short and muscular, their hooves so hard they had no need to be shod. If Angela had ever expected to see the epitome of a free spirit, it was in the Camargue horse.

"They're beautiful," she exclaimed. "But they're being rounded up. I thought they just roamed——"

"You're still living in the Dark Ages! Even the Camargue has become commercialized to a certain extent. These belong to the Vincennes estate. They take part in exhibitions for the tourists, and provide rides on nature trails. They're also a good workhorse. Château Vincennes is a working estate, Angela, not a luxury hideaway any more. Jacques is head of the magazine, as you know, and is away for much of the time with his own business in Paris. But the estate is run efficiently, both for tourism and stockbreeding, and the horses have to play their part in rounding up the bulls for slaughter and bull games. Every place of note has its arena and its bull games."

Every new bit of information fascinated her. She wanted to see everything, the bull games, and most of all the horses.

"Can we ride them?" she said eagerly. It was something she hadn't expected. Paul laughed.

"You think you'll be able to handle one of those?"

She looked at him indignantly. "You said there were tourist rides. I'm sure I'd be capable of *that.*"

"I'm sure you would." He was grinning now. His eyes glanced over her. "In fact, I'll look forward to seeing you on a horse. It's something Claudette would never do."

That definitely settled it then. At least it would be one activity where she wouldn't be in competition with the beautiful Claudette. The other girl's words spun into her mind.

"You haven't won yet . . ."

Angela felt a tremor run through her. All her pride was at stake. Claudette assumed, along with everyone else, that the engagement between her and Paul was genuine. This morning's papers had practically drooled over the way Paul had drawn her onto the stage with him last night. The pictures of them together showed them ecstatically happy, and there was no way she was going to give Claudette the satisfaction of thinking otherwise.

The charade only had to go on a little while. Once back in England the truth could be told, and a statement issued to the English papers that the wedding would not take place. There'd be no need for explanations. Angela couldn't stop the waves of bleakness washing over her at the thought, and deliberately stopped herself from thinking that far ahead.

She realized they were approaching a huge, magnificent mansion built in typical French style, and circled by a fringe of tall trees. Nowhere else in the world could there be such romantically situated châteaux, Angela thought with a little catch in her throat. Her gaze took in the leaded points of little turrets and circular towers set in weathered old stone, and the richly mullioned windows that caught the sheen of sunlight in a scarlet blaze of color. So much magnificence . . . it was suddenly overawing too, and as if Paul could read her mind, he put his hand over her own for a moment.

"Don't let it worry you, Angie. It looks very grand, but it's still someone's home, and Jacques is not the kind of man to put on airs, whatever his background."

"All the same, I'm glad I got to know him before I saw all this!" Angela said involuntarily.

Paul seemed to realize her apprehension was genuine, and his fingers curled round hers and squeezed them before he put his hands on the wheel.

"If you could face that theater audience last night, you can face anything," he said briefly. "And you're not alone, remember. You've got me by your side."

Angela felt the sudden saltiness of tears prickle her eyes. If only those words were prophetic. She wanted him by her side for always, not just for these last sweet days in the Camargue; but their time together was running out, and she still couldn't bear to think of all the days ahead without him.

Loving him as she did, her life would be utterly lonely, and infinitely dull. She wondered how she was going to survive with only the memories of these past weeks to last a lifetime. His music would always be at her disposal, but it was the man, and not his music, who had finally captured her heart.

Angela knew how foolish she had been to allow this mock engagement to go on. It was only prolonging a dream that could never become reality. But it was too late to retract now that the papers were so full of the romance that had happened in the country of love, and she must hang on to her senses a little while longer.

"I'll do my best not to let you down while we're here, Paul," she murmured now. "Though it's reasonable to suppose your personal assistant wasn't brought up in such regal surroundings, isn't it?"

"You're not accompanying me to Jacques's home as my personal assistant, but as my fiancée—or had you forgotten?" There was sudden tension in his voice. She couldn't be sure whether it was with annoyance or a temperamental aggression that she could possibly over-look the ring he had placed on her finger so recently.

"I'm hardly likely to forget," she said, unconsciously clenching her hands together so that the pressure of the ring dug into her.

Paul brought the car to a halt outside the main entrance to the château, put one finger beneath her chin and forced her to look at him. Angela swallowed. Was he really so blind that he couldn't see her love for him in her eyes? Or was she a more accomplished actress than she had ever thought possible?

"Do I push you too hard, my darling?" he said softly. "Sometimes when I look at you, it's hard for me to remember our engagement is a pretense at all."

"Is it?" she whispered. "But that's all it is, isn't it, Paul? A publicity stunt?"

She was torturing herself and she knew it. Forcing him to agree, as he must. Instead, he gave a short laugh, his finger curving round her cheek in a tender movement.

"Do I give such a bad impression of the newly engaged lover, Angela? I admit it's not a role of which I've had previous experience. But we both know there's no pretense in my desire for you. Who could blame me for wanting to take advantage of such a piquant situation as ours?"

He leaned across and touched the tip of her nose with his lips. In many ways it was as intimate a gesture as if he'd swept her into his arms. He spoke without the throb of passion in his voice that could so unnerve her without the brutal urgency of desire that she found so shamefully exciting. If this engagement had to end—as it did—she wished he could remain this tender and unemotional for the rest of the time they had together. It would be less wearing on her emotions, and in no way would it lessen her love for him.

They still sat enveloped in the intimacy of the moment when the huge oak door of the château opened and Jacques came running down the wide stone steps that were flanked by two enormous stone lions, a welcoming smile on his face. Behind him, Claudette Dubois waited in the doorway, elegant and startlingly beautiful in a black corduroy suit, with knee-length black boots and a vivid emerald green scarf tied around her neck. As Angela and Paul stepped out of the car to be greeted by Jacques, Claudette swept down toward them, totally ignoring Angela, and switching on all her voluptuous charm for Paul's sole benefit.

"*Chéri,* at last!" she trilled, as she linked her red-tipped hand through his arm. "I have been waiting with such impatience for your arrival. Never has time passed so slowly, but now you are here and all the black clouds have rolled away!"

It wasn't saying much for her host's company, Angela thought cynically, as she watched Claudette's full-lipped mouth smile provocatively into Paul's eyes. But Jacques clearly knew her well enough not to be offended, and smiled amiably at his new house guests, embracing them both.

"How can any man hope to compete when one look at the handsome Paul Blake can work such magic?" he said in a mock-mournful voice. "And we Frenchmen are reputed to be the world's most amorous lovers! I suppose you will contest that, Angela, since Paul is now your fiancé."

Angela felt the color rise in her cheeks, and didn't fail to notice the angry gleam in Claudette's lovely eyes. But it was gone in a moment as she linked her free arm through Jacques's now. The little movement effectively shut Angela out, as she was very well aware it was meant to.

"*Chéri,* you know I adore you!" Claudette hugged him to her side, "but Paul and I have always had a special fondness for each other that no one can ever touch."

As she finished speaking she turned with a start to look at Angela, an expression of dismay on her chiselled features. To the two men it must have looked completely natural, but to Angela it was glaringly calculated to embarrass her.

"Oh, *mon dieu,* what have I said? Angela, *chérie,* you must not take my words to mean anything significant! Say you forgive me if I have upset you at all, please!"

"Of course you haven't upset me," Angela said crisply, as Paul and Jacques turned to gauge her reaction. She squirmed inside, but she was determined not to let anybody see her anger, especially the sultry

Claudette. "I didn't expect Paul to have led a cloistered life before he met me, any more than I have!"

She saw Paul give the glimmer of a smile. She wished momentarily that Tim could have been as extravagant a character as Paul, instead of the rather lackluster bore that he was. Knowing instinctively just how inadequate she had found Tim's wooing, she grated her teeth as she heard the mocking note in Paul's response.

"Angela's not the jealous type," he told Claudette. "A good thing, with some of the ladies she has to deal with at the stage door."

"And you and I know all about those, don't we, *chéri?*" Claudette said archly, establishing an immediate intimacy between them.

Claudette knew exactly what she was doing, Angela thought savagely. She wondered if Paul really thought she was without jealousy as she watched the two of them walk inside the huge château, with Jacques gallantly waiting for her to follow them. Jealousy raged through her like a flame as she saw Paul put his arm lightly round the singer's curving waist and squeeze it gently.

Once inside the mansion, coffee and petit fours were immediately served by smoothly efficient staff. Angela could see only too well what Claudette was trying to do. She chose to dismiss Angela as if she were of no importance, despite the fact that Angela wore the antique engagement ring on her finger.

Once coffee was finished, Jacques held out his hand to Angela.

"Come, *chérie,* and I'll give you a guided tour of my home. Paul has seen it many times before, so while he and Claudette relive these old memories you and I will become the tourists for an hour or so."

It was hardly calculated to calm her nerves, but there was no objection she could make, and she rose at once, not missing the triumphant smile on Claudette's face as she left the room with Jacques. Unwittingly, he had played right into her hands, Angela thought. Though why should she care? The sudden depressing thought swept over her. It wasn't as if she was Paul's *real* wife-to-be. If she was, nothing on earth would have let her leave the two of them alone together for Claudette to play her own game.

As she followed Jacques through the maze of corridors of the château, with its marbled floors and costly furnishings, half her mind was still in the room where she had left Paul and Claudette. She occasionally heard the ripple of Claudette's rich laughter. She tried hard to pay attention to all that Jacques was telling her, and any other time she'd have been enchanted with the elegance and charm of such a fine old French building. They reached the armory, with its grisly reminders of the past, including suits of armor, muskets, and the great swords that adorned the walls with pictures of past generations of the *famille* Vincennes. Suddenly Jacques looked at her quizzically.

"Do I get the impression that your mind isn't fully on me, Angela?" His voice was light, and she flushed with embarrassment.

"I'm sorry, Jacques. It's terribly interesting, and you must think I'm being very rude——"

"Not at all. Just in love," he spoke with the understanding of a Frenchman, and to Angela's horror, her eyes suddenly misted over. Jacques put his arms on her shoulders, looking searchingly into her eyes.

"My dear girl, what have I said? It's perfectly natural to be thinking more about your future husband than old suits of armor!"

"I wonder if Paul is thinking about me," she muttered, despite herself. "I doubt it, with Claudette making it so obvious that Paul's still number one in her life."

She couldn't bear to think of the delightful re-

170

miniscences the two of them might be sharing right now. Wondering if Paul was regretting the crazy engagement announcement, and glad that he could soon be out of it. She wondered if he was confiding the truth of it all to Claudette, in yet one more shared intimacy. She drew in her breath as the pain of it washed over her.

Jacques pressed a soft kiss to her cheek. "You are a goose, *ma petite*. Claudette means nothing to Paul except as an old friend, and she is being a little naughty perhaps, to tease you. It's just her way. But surely it's obvious that it's you who are number one in Paul's life, as you put it! Anyone with half an eye in his head can see that he's in love with you."

Angela swallowed painfully at his confident words. He tipped her chin up to look deeper into her eyes in just the way Paul did.

"Angela, Paul has always been a proud man, even a little possessive of his own success. Deservedly so, and it's something common to many artists that the rest of us don't always recognize. But last night he shared everything with you in his announcement after the concert. It was his gift, and perhaps only those who know him well realize what a gift it was. I think you're making problems where there are none, *chérie!*"

She forced herself to nod, murmuring that it was no doubt the strain of the tour that was making her jittery.

"Of course," Jacques said at once. "But now you can unwind and enjoy our lovely countryside, and all your fears will be unfounded. And you must meet our other house guests later. We are eight in all, and I know you will enjoy talking with Sally Colbert, who is a compatriot of yours. She and her husband, Pierre, live in Arles, and Sally came here for a holiday twenty years ago, fell in love with Pierre and the Camargue, and has stayed ever since. I warn you, *chérie*, such tales are undoubtedly the stuff of which the Camargue is made!"

She was laughing with him as he teased her, and then he said something else to lighten her mood as they made their way back down the wide curving staircase.

"I have just remembered, Angela. There are some letters for you in the drawing room. The English postmarks should put you in good spirits. I'll show you to the drawing room and you can read them at your leisure."

It was quite a relief to be on her own for a short while, Angela realized, as Jacques closed the tall doors of the drawing room behind him. The two letters had been placed on a silver salver, and she looked eagerly at the handwriting on each envelope. One was from Lorna, the other from Tim. She tore Lorna's open eagerly, knowing it would be like a breath of home to read her old flatmate's enthusiastic chatter. As soon as she started reading she discovered that Lorna—and everybody in the country by the sound of it—had heard about her and Paul, and most of the letter referred to Angela's romantic engagement:

The papers took up the story over here. You can expect a royal welcome when you get back. I'm dying to know if you've set the date yet—and can I be bridesmaid?"

It went on in the same tone. Angela bit her lip as she came to the end. She had always hated deceit, and had never expected to be party to such a gigantic deception as this.

Lorna finished with a brief mention of Tim:

By the way, Tim's all right. He's been round to supper a couple of times. No, there's nothing in it, but he seems to get on pretty well with my new flatmate. Did I tell you about her? She's in computers—frighteningly intelligent . . .

Well, hadn't she wanted Tim to get over her? She hadn't expected it *quite* so quickly, Angela thought ruefully. She opened his letter. He certainly didn't give the impression of having a broken heart. She was glad, except that it gave her an oddly empty feeling. When she parted from Paul, she'd need someone to lean on for a while, and Tim had always been there before. She told herself she was being completely unfair to him, but it didn't help. The emptiness still persisted.

Paul and Claudette came in while she was still reading. The singer clung to his arm as if she couldn't stand up by herself. Angela felt herself bristle.

"Letters from home?" Claudette said sweetly.

"That's right. From my former flatmate. And one from an old friend—Tim." Her eyes were on Paul as she spoke. Suddenly she wanted to make him feel as jealous as she did right now when he stood there so blatantly with Claudette hanging onto him as if she owned him. His eyes flickered, but it was Claudette who laughed triumphantly.

"You see, my darling?" she spoke directly to Paul, her voice low and husky. "Old ties are hard to break, no? You and Angela should take time to get to know each other before you rush into marriage."

So they had been discussing it, had they? Angela felt her anger rise. His reply astounded her as he patted Claudette's hand.

"And as I told you, *chérie,* I know all I need to know about my fiancée. We'll be married as soon as we get back to England—unless I can persuade her to stay on here a little longer and get married by special license. I think the Camargue has touched her romantic heart."

Angela jumped to her feet. She kept her temper with an effort, aware that Jacques was bringing in the two guests from Arles to introduce.

"I think I'd like to be consulted before outsiders get to hear of my wedding date," she said in a tight voice.

"Unless you were thinking of informing the papers without telling me?"

She turned her back on him, her eyes blazing, and she heard him give an explicit oath before he strode out of the room in his old arrogant manner. What on earth had he expected? Angela seethed. He thought he could do just as he pleased, making such an outrageous announcement as this last one! Well, he'd learn that she had no intention of being anyone's puppet! Her heart thudded in her chest, and she hardly realized that she and Claudette were alone for the first time until she caught the other girl's movement as she leaned back in a silk-covered chair to gaze at Angela through smoldering eyes.

About the only thing to mollify Angela was that tight-set expression on Claudette's lovely face. His words had clearly been a shock to her after the way she'd been throwing herself at him. But now they were alone, the chips were down, and Claudette made no secret of the way she felt.

"Tell me how you've managed it," she said insultingly. "Other girls have tried to lure Paul into marriage, but none has ever succeeded——"

Angela reddened angrily. "There was no question of luring him, as you so delicately put it." She saw no need to choose her words carefully any longer. "Though maybe you've never heard of love——"

Claudette laughed. "Love! My dear little ingenue, I know all about love. So does Paul—but I wonder why he had to take things this far!" She looked Angela up and down with measured derision. "Of course, the whole thing is a mistake. You must see that! An artist of Paul's caliber needs someone of similar temperament to share his life. Someone who understands the highs and lows of the artistic temperament, and is completely compatible——"

"Someone like you, I suppose?" There was no

174

pretense now. All the animosity between them sparked like electric shock waves. Claudette's eyes glittered.

"There is no one *like* me, *chérie*. I am unique. Artists are as individual as the stars; which is why the popular press give us that ridiculous label. But this marriage—" she gave an expressive shrug—"even if it comes to pass, it won't last. Paul is a perfectionist. He needs perfection in his life, and in his wife. He needs another *artiste*, not a paid assistant. You do not even know him! How can you know what goes to make up such a man? His special needs, his moods, his *scars*. You are quite the wrong person to share his life, little English Angela."

Claudette finished with a crushing little burst of venom. But Angela was only listening to one part of her tirade. All she heard was the reference to Paul's scars, about which he was so sensitive. Her face, that had been so suffused with color, seemed to feel drained now, and as if Claudette knew exactly the effect her words had had, she gave a taunting smile. As if to emphasize the fact to Angela that she had personal knowledge of Paul Blake . . . very personal knowledge indeed.

Chapter Eleven

It didn't matter how many times Angela told herself it was pointless to feel such stinging jealousy. Claudette managed to imply in so many ways that she and Paul had been lovers in the past and would be again, whether he was married or not. She dismissed the idea of his marriage as entirely incidental. It wouldn't affect the great love of his life, namely Claudette Dubois.

Why didn't he marry *her* then? Jacques had given her the answer once—their careers were too important to both of them. Angela tried to feel contempt. No career in the world was worth losing the love of a lifetime. But in Claudette's constant innuendoes in the next days whenever she managed to get Angela alone, she never failed to add more fuel to the flame, and to smile seductively up into Paul's eyes at every opportunity.

She'd tell him with a pretty little pout that there might not be many more times like this when she could monopolize him a little, and she was sure dear Angela would understand. Angela understood only too well, and so did Paul, she realized furiously. He was enjoying the situation, naturally. With two adoring women hovering around him, what more could he ask?

Château Vincennes had a reputation for hospitality. They were a mixed set of guests who were interesting and lively. Angela discounted Claudette from her thoughts. The cuisine was of a high standard, with succulent red beef from Vincennes stock, and the frothiest soufflés Angela had ever tasted. And most evenings after dinner, Paul agreed to play for them. He didn't need much persuasion. He was relaxed now at the end of the tour, and among friends. To Angela he seemed to be playing a waiting game. It puzzled her. It was as if he really believed they were going to be married, as if he was sure of her, and he could afford to flirt with Claudette, his old friend . . . who never tired of darting triumphant looks at "little English Angela."

But she became as absorbed as everyone else when Paul's music filled the elegant rooms of the old château. The pieces were all familiar to her now, Debussy and Chopin, the intricacies of Mendelssohn's "Spring Song," and the softer Brahms waltzes. But he never played "Autumn Leaves," to Angela's relief. She couldn't bear to hear him playing her song while Claudette leaned across the piano watching him so adoringly.

It was like a scene in a musical show, Angela thought on the second evening when it followed the same pattern. The handsome pianist in formal evening dress, smiling into the dark eyes of the beautiful singer, stunning in a gown of clinging red silk. The rest of them gathered around the room were merely extras, including herself. Earlier, Paul had told her she looked beautiful. She wore a gown of silvery white, and the antique ring glittered on her engagement finger, but beside Claudette, every woman in the room paled.

Finally she could bear it no longer. It was already quite late, and coffee and biscuits had been served by an unobtrusive maid. But no one seemed to want the evening to end. She spoke quickly to Jacques.

"Would you mind if I go to my room, Jacques? I have rather a headache."

"Of course not, *chérie*. Can I get you anything?"

"No, thank you. I have some tablets." She forced a smile at Paul and the rest of them. "Excuse me, please. I'll see you all in the morning."

Paul rose at once from the piano and kissed her

lightly on the cheek, for the benefit of the others, or because he knew she could hardly move away from his embrace.

"I'll look in and see you later, darling," he murmured.

"I'll be asleep——"

"If you are, I won't disturb you," he said steadily, daring her to make a scene. Out of the corner of her eye she saw Claudette watching them, and impulsively she put her arms round Paul's neck and kissed him properly. It was a bittersweet moment, but she couldn't help herself.

No one thought it at all odd for her to kiss her fiancé in front of them all, but it left her knees a little weak as she found her way through the old corridors to her own room. She hadn't intended to invite him to her room, she merely wanted to irritate Claudette. She was beginning to think that she'd been a bit feeble in running out on them. Inventing a headache was about as feeble as you could get! And anyway, now she'd left the field wide open for Claudette. She was too tense to sleep, and she wasn't really tired.

Outside, through the screen of trees, she could hear the constant moan of the mistral and the occasional whinnying of the wild white horses. It was eerie and yet hauntingly evocative. The Camargue was seemingly so bleak and uninviting, and yet it teemed with life and appealed to the senses. Though not to everyone's, she supposed: probably not to Claudette's. Take away the glamor of the Château Vincennes and Jacques's fortune, and she had no doubt Claudette would be heading back for the bright lights of Paris.

The sound of the piano broke through her thoughts again. Angela's room was directly above the drawing room where the rest of them were, and then she heard Claudette's rich tones accompanying Paul's music. They performed half a dozen songs together, and with each one Angela became more depressed, especially because she knew she'd brought all this on herself. If she hadn't been so prudish, by now she and Paul . . .

She'd be his mistress, she thought bitterly. He had no intention of marrying her, regardless of the stories he gave out to the press. It was just a publicity gimmick, and it had worked like a charm. But it wasn't his mistress she wanted to be. She closed her eyes a moment against the sweet storm of desire coursing through her at the thought. But it wasn't his *mistress* she wanted to be, it was his wife. And she wanted him to love her, love her, as wildly and ecstatically as she loved him. But he didn't know the meaning of the word.

She discovered she really did have a headache now. She'd brought that on herself too, she thought ruefully. But she'd never sleep. She slid her arms out of the silvery gown and hung it up carefully, and after a moment's hesitation, she put on a blouse and skirt. She didn't want to invite trouble by being undressed if Paul came knocking on her door.

She picked up the two letters from home, and reread them a couple of times. She might as well answer them, and because she'd always been honest with Lorna, she couldn't bear to keep up the pretense any longer. At least with one person in the world, she had to have complete honesty. She wrote at length, swearing her friend to secrecy—but in any case this farce of an engagement would probably be over by the time Lorna received the letter, so what did it matter?

So you see, your desire to be a bridesmaid was a bit like rubbing salt in the wound. I wouldn't tell this to anyone else, but I love him so much it's driving me crazy. I didn't know it was possible to love someone so much— and he only sees me as one more woman to add to his collection. I'm so vulnerable when he's around, Lorna. Me, the so-efficient P.R.O.! Isn't there some saying about death being the great leveler? I'd say that applies to love too. If he only knew how often I've been tempted to throw away my pride—but you know me. Always the stickler for detail. And while there's the little detail of Paul not loving me, I guess we've come to an impasse. Forgive me for unburdening all this on you, but now it's nearly over, I realize it's been more of a strain than I thought. Nearly over . . . I can't go on this way, but I just can't imagine life without him either. That's the hell of it. See you soon—and remember, not a word. I'm trusting you.

She signed it quickly. She knew Lorna could be trusted, but she hadn't intended to put quite so much on paper. Once started, though, the words just poured out, and in a strange way she felt somehow cleaner. She glanced at Tim's letter, but she couldn't face writing to him after all. He musn't know the truth, of course, and she wasn't in the mood to write trite phrases that meant nothing. She felt too emotional, and suddenly claustrophobic, despite the vast room and the beauty of her surroundings. She felt the need to be outside, to feel the wind in her hair and the cool night air on her cheeks.

She slipped out of her room and down the stairs. There was no more singing from the drawing room now and the piano had stopped. The party was probably breaking up for the night. When Paul knocked on her door and got no answer, she hoped he'd assume she was asleep. The wind had softened just a little. It sighed through the trees now, and the leaves swirled round her feet. In the last days summer had subtly given way to autumn, at least here where the leaves made a soft carpet of red and gold. Angela bit her lips. The autumn leaves . . .

Her taut nerves relaxed a little as she strolled around the old château, discreetly lit by night by hidden lights among the shrubs. There was no need to be afraid, and she realized how much she needed this time alone. She seemed to be surrounded with people all the time, and all of them affecting her in different ways.

Claudette with her taunts and her flaunting ways whenever Paul was near; the two Vincennes cousins, anxious that everyone should be enjoying themselves and pushing hospitality to holiday camp proportions; the couple from Arles, charmed that she and Paul should have found "love" so suddenly; Jacques, clearly thinking what a scoop it would be for his magazine if the happy couple would stay on and be married under his own roof. For a moment Angela imagined the lovely old château as the setting for a wedding, and swallowed the lump in her throat at the sweetness of the thought.

For once she wasn't certain of Paul's mood. She understood him immediately when he was arrogant and chauvinistic. She could cope with his temperament. She even managed to overcome her weakness when he exerted all his male charisma toward her and showed just how tender a lover he could be. But right now he seemed strangely withdrawn when she happened to be alone with him, almost as if he'd given up on her.

Angela shivered. She should be glad, but she knew how desperately empty life would be without him, and how much richer her life had become because of him. Even the moods and the artistic temperament added a bonus to her life that she would miss beyond imagination.

As if to echo her sudden depression, she heard the distant roar of galloping hooves and the haunting whinnying of a score of wild horses. She imagined them silhouetted against the indigo skyline, white manes flowing free, muscles rippling, free as the wind. Then there was another roar, a rumble of thunder cracking above, and distantly a jagged streak of lightning lit the sky. It would probably be an electrical storm somewhere, since there was no sign of rain; but the first clap of thunder had Angela rooted to the spot for a moment. Ridiculously, she had always had an irrational fear of thunder.

She was too far from the château to reach it before another jagged streak of lightning lit the horizon. Gasping a little, she looked around in terror. She was very near the stables, and without hesitation she began running toward them, to slip inside the safety of their protective walls until the dry storm passed over. And almost at once she realized her mistake.

Perhaps it was the sound of their free companions thundering across the marshes that had startled the stabled Vincennes horses. Or the sound of her running footsteps, coupled with her gasping breaths that began the restless stamping and snorting. She looked in sudden fright at the squat white heads and short bodies that seemed to be crowding her. Jacques had assured her they were as tamed as their free spirits would ever be.

Angela tried to speak to the horses, but her voice was harsh in her throat, and would do nothing to soothe or reassure them. Perhaps the electrical storm upset them too. Whatever the reason, the animal nearest her suddenly reared up, his hooves flailing toward her. She staggered back against the wall of the stable with a sharp scream of real fear.

There was nowhere else for her to go since she had moved right inside the stable to be as far as possible from the elements outside. She found herself trapped against the wall with the two horses in the stall pawing the ground in agitation. They were no longer the romantic animals of her imagination, but a real threat to her safety. And the ironic thing was, the storm outside seemed to have passed on as quickly as it had appeared, with only a rumbling of distant thunder to be heard. Above it, she was all too aware of the thunderous beating of her heart as she fought to calm the restless horses.

"It's all right," she stuttered, her eyes never leaving them. Wasn't it best to keep staring them straight in the eyes? Nobody told you how unnerving it was though, with the horses' eyes rolling in their heads, and that hideous snorting sound coming from their throats. "I shan't hurt you . . ."

That was ironic, too. When it came to the crunch, they were the masters after all, these creatures of the wilds. She screamed as the two horses lurched against each other and stamped viciously at the ground, sending up clouds of dry dusty straw, which dried up Angela's mouth and throat. And then to her blessed relief, she heard the sound of running footsteps. She went limp as she saw Paul's tall figure filling the doorway of the stable.

"Thank God," Angela croaked. "They won't let me go——"

It was like a crazy nightmare, to be trapped by two wild white horses. They were tethered, but she had no doubt that if they became really frenzied they'd break loose.

Paul was talking to them gently now, telling her to get outside. She saw them turn on him for a moment, and he swore loudly. Her one thought then was for his hands—his beautiful hands—but the fright was leaving the animals and they gradually quieted. By then two stable lads had appeared, but assured that everything was under control, they went sleepily back to bed and let the crazy Englishman deal with the situation.

Finally Paul turned to Angela, who stood white-faced against the outside wall of the stable.

"Are you hurt?" he said roughly.

She shook her head.

"Then what the hell were you doing here? I saw you wandering about just before I went upstairs——"

The weak tears rushed to Angela's eyes. After the shock of the past ten minutes, she couldn't bear for him to speak to her in that harsh voice. She felt as if her knees were going to buckle under her. As if he thought the same, he suddenly grabbed her arms and held her up. Her heart was beating wildly under the thin shirt she wore.

"This wind is chilly. There's an empty stall next door to this one. Come inside a minute until you calm down."

She followed him obediently. It was still part of the nightmare. But inside the stall there was a soft bed of fresh hay, and Angela sank down on it. He sat down beside her.

"Why—why did you come after me?" she asked in a muffled voice. The sting of tears was still close to the surface, and the last thing she wanted to do was break down and cry all over him.

"I went up to your room to fetch a jacket for you. I knew you'd underestimate the chill of the night. I'm afraid I dropped it somewhere on the path when I heard you scream."

Paul's controlled voice suddenly stopped and with a sharp oath he pulled her into the circle of his arms.

"Don't ever do that to me again, do you hear?" he grated.

"To *you!* What about me? I was the one who was in danger!" Angela gasped. Still the egotist, she raged inside.

"When you love somebody the way you profess to love me, then you owe them something, and that includes not scaring me half to death by screaming in the night——"

Angela didn't let him go on. Her white face flooded with color as she beat against his chest to free herself, but his grip was like iron.

"You read my letter to Lorna! How dare you! It was private and personal, and you had no right——"

His tone was masterful, as arrogant as she'd ever heard it now.

"I have every right, though I must admit I don't

184

make a habit of reading other people's letters. But when it's left open and I catch sight of my name and various other interesting little bits of information, I could hardly resist the temptation. I'm no saint, sweet Angela!"

Oh, that he wasn't! Even now, his hands were wandering up and down her bare arms, sending the treacherous little tingles through her body. And the wanton desire she tried so hard to deny was flaming over her as his lips began their exploration of her mouth and throat. She twisted away from him, but this time he had no intention of letting her go.

"Why don't you give all your attentions to Claudette?" she burst out. "You've hardly been resisting her flirtations since we've been here, have you? And I'm sure she'd be agreeable to carry on from where you left off—if you ever *did* leave off."

"What in God's name are you babbling about?" Paul paused in the subtle unbuttoning of her shirt to gaze into her tortured hazel eyes, glowing like amber gems in the soft light from the château grounds.

"You and Claudette," Angela said faintly. What he was doing now was almost making her dizzy. She dragged her thoughts together. "She as good as told me you and she had been—been—she described the scars on your back so eloquently."

Angela felt the laughter on his lips against the softness of her breast. It was the reaction she'd have expected, she thought, though it was hard to feel cynical when his tongue was doing such delightful things to her.

"And how do you suppose she knew about them, my angel?" Paul's voice teased her. "Claudette has a knack for making people see things the way she'd like them to be. But if it makes you feel any better, she and I have never been lovers. I'm not denying there have been women in my life, but Claudette's knowledge of my imperfections came the way yours did—on a beach!"

"Oh!" It was so obvious the word came out in an embarrassed whisper. She suddenly realized her small relaxation had given Paul the signal to take more advantage of the soft cocoon of hay that enveloped them in its dry sweetness. His long hard body was covering hers now, moving sensuously against her thighs. She wanted him so much. She gave a little nervous laugh at the incongruity of his appearance, in the once immaculate evening clothes that were now dusty and creased.

"Your clothes," she murmured dizzily.

"There's an easy answer to that!" He had shrugged out of his jacket before she could protest that wasn't what she'd meant at all.

"Isn't it about time we both said what we mean, Angie?" He kissed the tip of her nose while his hand stroked her golden skin in a way that inflamed every nerve with longing. "I've never known such a contrary woman, but maybe that's partly what makes you so exciting to me—and what makes me love you and want you so badly."

Angela's eyes blurred over. It was what she had longed to hear for so long, and he knew it! He'd read her letter to Lorna, and words were easy to say. They were the barrier he hadn't realized existed between them, and she still couldn't quite believe they were true. Suddenly his lips left her breasts, where they seemed to wander so instinctively, and the seductive voice became more tender than she'd ever heard it. Tender and a little halting, surprisingly so for a man like Paul. He held her close to him, where she could feel the wild thudding of his heart, as vibrant as her own.

"There have been other women, darling Angie, and I'm not denying it. But I've never told any woman I loved her until now. I've wanted them and enjoyed them, but love was always such a scarce commodity in my younger days that it was something too precious in my mind to talk about lightly. I could never say the words until they meant I was offering my heart and soul just to one woman."

She clung to him, unable to say anything. His words were sweet, sweet music to her ears.

"How long have you felt like that?" she whispered finally. "Before the—engagement?"

Paul gave a rueful laugh.

"My God, what a swine you must have thought me all these weeks, Angie. I thought I could storm my way into your life without any mention of love. I was expecting somebody else to do all the giving as usual, and I'd do the taking. I didn't even recognize my feelings as love. I just knew I had to have you. It gave me a good feeling to see you wearing my mother's ring, and to see our photos in the papers together. I didn't even realize I was fooling myself into thinking it was all true, until it dawned on me that these few days were really the end. You'd made no concessions to me at all, but when I saw you in that stable tonight, pinned against the wall, I knew I'd move heaven and earth rather than lose you."

"And besides, you'd already seen my letter to Lorna," she murmured.

"Yes I had," he admitted. "And maybe it was the trigger I needed. I only knew that reading your words was like the opening of a flood gate for me. Knowing that you loved me, and that what I'd felt for you all along was love, pure and simple. I love you, Angie. I don't think I'll ever tire of telling you now."

She wasn't too sure that his love was sincere, now that his passion was aroused again. But she was past resisting. Why resist, when her passion was soaring to meet his so exultantly?

She slipped her small hands inside his silky shirt, experimenting with her palms against the hard texture of his chest, with its mesh of dark hair. She heard his indrawn breath.

"It seems to be a day for 'firsts,' doesn't it, Paul?"

she said huskily. His mouth touched hers in a long sweet kiss. It told her that in love there was nothing to fear. That he could be as gentle as a summer's breeze.

"It's the first time I've ever asked anyone to marry me, too," he murmured against her mouth. "And this time I'm asking you properly, my darling. No cameras, no gimmicks, no publicity stunt. I want you to be my wife, Angie, more than anything in the world, and I'd like it to be here. The château would be a marvelous setting for a wedding, and you'll be such a beautiful bride. But it's your choice."

He was almost—humble! The thought sent a delicious little shiver running through her. And her answer had a double meaning they both understood as her eager arms pulled him down to her.

"Let it be here," she whispered, as love's sweet music took them to a crescendo of happiness that had only just begun.

Genuine Silhouette sterling silver bookmark for only $15.95!

What a beautiful way to hold your place in your current romance! This genuine sterling silver bookmark, with the distinctive Silhouette symbol in elegant black, measures 1½" long and 1" wide. It makes a beautiful gift for yourself, and for every romantic you know! And, at only $15.95 each, including all postage and handling charges, you'll want to order several now, while supplies last.

Send your name and address with check or money order for $15.95 per bookmark ordered to
**Simon & Schuster Enterprises
120 Brighton Rd., P.O. Box 5020
Clifton, N.J. 07012
Attn: Bookmark**

Bookmarks can be ordered pre-paid only. No charges will be accepted. Please allow 4-6 weeks for delivery.

N.Y. State Residents
Please Add Sales Tax

Silhouette Romance

IT'S YOUR OWN SPECIAL TIME
Contemporary romances for today's women.
Each month, six very special love stories will be yours
from SILHOUETTE. Look for them wherever books are sold
or order now from the coupon below.

$1.50 each

☐ 5 Goforth	☐ 28 Hampson	☐ 54 Beckman	☐ 83 Halston
☐ 6 Stanford	☐ 29 Wildman	☐ 55 LaDame	☐ 84 Vitek
☐ 7 Lewis	☐ 30 Dixon	☐ 56 Trent	☐ 85 John
☐ 8 Beckman	☐ 32 Michaels	☐ 57 John	☐ 86 Adams
☐ 9 Wilson	☐ 33 Vitek	☐ 58 Stanford	☐ 87 Michaels
☐ 10 Caine	☐ 34 John	☐ 59 Vernon	☐ 88 Stanford
☐ 11 Vernon	☐ 35 Stanford	☐ 60 Hill	☐ 89 James
☐ 17 John	☐ 38 Browning	☐ 61 Michaels	☐ 90 Major
☐ 19 Thornton	☐ 39 Sinclair	☐ 62 Halston	☐ 92 McKay
☐ 20 Fulford	☐ 46 Stanford	☐ 63 Brent	☐ 93 Browning
☐ 22 Stephens	☐ 47 Vitek	☐ 71 Ripy	☐ 94 Hampson
☐ 23 Edwards	☐ 48 Wildman	☐ 73 Browning	☐ 95 Wisdom
☐ 24 Healy	☐ 49 Wisdom	☐ 76 Hardy	☐ 96 Beckman
☐ 25 Stanford	☐ 50 Scott	☐ 78 Oliver	☐ 97 Clay
☐ 26 Hastings	☐ 52 Hampson	☐ 81 Roberts	☐ 98 St. George
☐ 27 Hampson	☐ 53 Browning	☐ 82 Dailey	☐ 99 Camp

$1.75 each

☐ 100 Stanford	☐ 110 Trent	☐ 120 Carroll	☐ 130 Hardy
☐ 101 Hardy	☐ 111 South	☐ 121 Langan	☐ 131 Stanford
☐ 102 Hastings	☐ 112 Stanford	☐ 122 Scofield	☐ 132 Wisdom
☐ 103 Cork	☐ 113 Browning	☐ 123 Sinclair	☐ 133 Rowe
☐ 104 Vitek	☐ 114 Michaels	☐ 124 Beckman	☐ 134 Charles
☐ 105 Eden	☐ 115 John	☐ 125 Bright	☐ 135 Logan
☐ 106 Dailey	☐ 116 Lindley	☐ 126 St. George	☐ 136 Hampson
☐ 107 Bright	☐ 117 Scott	☐ 127 Roberts	☐ 137 Hunter
☐ 108 Hampson	☐ 118 Dailey	☐ 128 Hampson	☐ 138 Wilson
☐ 109 Vernon	☐ 119 Hampson	☐ 129 Converse	☐ 139 Vitek

$1.75 each

☐ 140 Erskine	☐ 158 Reynolds	☐ 175 Jarrett	☐ 192 John
☐ 142 Browning	☐ 159 Tracy	☐ 176 Vitek	☐ 193 Trent
☐ 143 Roberts	☐ 160 Hampson	☐ 177 Dailey	☐ 194 Barry
☐ 144 Goforth	☐ 161 Trent	☐ 178 Hampson	☐ 195 Dailey
☐ 145 Hope	☐ 162 Ashby	☐ 179 Beckman	☐ 196 Hampson
☐ 146 Michaels	☐ 163 Roberts	☐ 180 Roberts	☐ 197 Summers
☐ 147 Hampson	☐ 164 Browning	☐ 181 Terrill	☐ 198 Hunter
☐ 148 Cork	☐ 165 Young	☐ 182 Clay	☐ 199 Roberts
☐ 149 Saunders	☐ 166 Wisdom	☐ 183 Stanley	☐ 200 Lloyd
☐ 150 Major	☐ 167 Hunter	☐ 184 Hardy	☐ 201 Starr
☐ 151 Hampson	☐ 168 Carr	☐ 185 Hampson	☐ 202 Hampson
☐ 152 Halston	☐ 169 Scott	☐ 186 Howard	☐ 203 Browning
☐ 153 Dailey	☐ 170 Ripy	☐ 187 Scott	☐ 204 Carroll
☐ 154 Beckman	☐ 171 Hill	☐ 188 Cork	☐ 205 Maxam
☐ 155 Hampson	☐ 172 Browning	☐ 189 Stephens	☐ 206 Manning
☐ 156 Sawyer	☐ 173 Camp	☐ 190 Hampson	☐ 207 Windham
☐ 157 Vitek	☐ 174 Sinclair	☐ 191 Browning	

$1.95 each

_#208 SUNSET IN PARADISE Halston	_#214 LOVE SO RARE Hampson
_#209 TRAIL OF THE UNICORN LaDame	_#215 HER MOTHER'S KEEPER Roberts
_#210 FLIGHT OF FANCY Eden	_#216 LOVE'S SWEET MUSIC Saunders
_#211 GREEK IDYLL Walters	_#217 BLUE MIST OF MORNING Vitek
_#212 YESTERDAY'S PROMISE Young	_#218 FOUNTAINS OF PARADISE Hunter
_#213 SEPARATE CABINS Dailey	_#219 ISLAND SPELL Cork

**Look for _WESTERN MAN_ by Janet Dailey
available in June and
LOST IN LOVE by Mia Maxam in July.**

SILHOUETTE BOOKS, Department SB/1

1230 Avenue of the Americas
New York, NY 10020

Please send me the books I have checked above. I am enclosing $_____
(please add 50¢ to cover postage and handling. NYS and NYC residents please
add appropriate sales tax). Send check or money order—no cash or C.O.D.s
please. Allow six weeks for delivery.

NAME _____

ADDRESS _____

CITY _____ STATE/ZIP _____

Coming next month from
Silhouette Romances

The Dawn Is Golden by Anne Hampson

Melanie believed her only means of escape was to flee with Vidas Loudaros to his Greek island. Once there she found herself faced with trading her innocence for freedom!

Practical Dreamer by Dixie Browning

Thane Coulter shattered Tally's poised professional front whenever he came near, and yet, he was the only man who could pick up all the pieces.

Two Faces Of Love by Mary Carroll

Marcello's insistent love-making had dazzled Gina, but his enigmatic behavior was breaking her heart. Gina realized too late that she was in love with a man who didn't need her.

A Private Eden by Ashley Summers

Upset that Gabe had deceived her, Sara no longer knew what to think about the man she found so seductively attractive . . . but who continued to elude her love.

Hidden Isle by Ruth Langan

Morgan was capable, sincere, and in love with screenwriter Kent Taylor. Alone with him on his Canadian island retreat, she longed to show Kent her love—before he left the island and her life forever.

Delta River Magic by Edith St. George

Powerless to say no to Chase Barrister, her handsome, enigmatic boss, Francine accompanied his godmother on a cruise down the Mississippi. Only Francine didn't realize she'd be accompanying Chase as well!